THE HOUSE UPTOWN

Also by Melissa Ginsburg

Sunset City
Dear Weather Ghost

THE HOUSE UPTOWN

MELISSA GINSBURG

FLATIRON
BOOKS
NEW YORK

THE HOUSE UPTOWN. Copyright © 2021 by Melissa Ginsburg. All rights reserved. Printed in the United States of America. For information, address Flatiron Books, 120 Broadway, New York, NY 10271.

www.flatironbooks.com

Design by Donna Sinisgalli Noetzel

The Library of Congress Cataloging-in-Publication Data is available upon request.

ISBN 978-1-250-78418-6 (hardcover)
ISBN 978-1-250-78419-3 (ebook)

Our books may be purchased in bulk for promotional, educational, or business use. Please contact your local bookseller or the Macmillan Corporate and Premium Sales Department at 1-800-221-7945, extension 5442, or by email at MacmillanSpecialMarkets@macmillan.com.

First Edition: 2021

10 9 8 7 6 5 4 3 2 1

For my parents, Betsy and Guss

And in memory of my grandmothers,
Jake Hinds Allee
and
Carol Mantinband Ginsburg

THE HOUSE UPTOWN

PROLOGUE

1997

Lane came awake to the sound of unoiled hinges, her heart pumping hard. She had been dreaming of a massive cloud, a storm that blew all the doors open, dread billowing around her.

She struggled to wrench herself from the panic of the dream. The clock read 2:30. She inhaled deeply, lay still, willing her body to relax. She listened to the house settle, visualized her daughter Louise tucked safely in bed down the hall. Lane was almost back asleep when she heard a sound that shouldn't be there—footsteps? Voices? Lane's arms tingled, her heart pounded again. She sat up in bed, reached for the light, froze at the distinct soft thud of the kitchen door closing.

Swiftly Lane shoved her feet into slippers and went to the bedroom door, opened it, listened again. What was Louise up to, sneaking out in the middle of the night? Or sneaking in a boy? At seventeen, it was the age for those shenanigans. Lane would have to ground her, the whole house would be tense and awful, it would be impossible to get any work done. Lane thought of her upcoming deadlines—she was already behind schedule, and this would make it worse. Irritation replaced the fear she had felt a moment ago.

She heard a voice again, coming from the kitchen. A man's voice. Who the hell was Louise mixed up with? She crept down the hall toward the kitchen, listening. The man spoke again, though she couldn't make out the words. She heard someone answer, not her daughter. Burglars. At least two of them.

She walked fast, careful to avoid the creaks in the old hardwoods. She made her way toward her daughter's bedroom at the front of the house. As she passed the mantel she grabbed a heavy brass candlestick, carried it at her side. She wished for a better weapon, but her gun was locked up in the hall closet, she'd never get to it in time. More important to get Louise away from them, out of the house.

She would wake Louise and they would run out the front door, it was the closest. Lane tried to remember if the key was in the lock, or in her purse—where had she left it? Her skin prickled everywhere, her grip tightened on the candlestick. She could still hear, faintly, the men in the kitchen.

She was almost to the front hall, almost to Louise, when she mis-stepped, hit the treads too hard. The floor creaked. The voices behind her stopped. Lane looked toward the kitchen. A man stepped into the hall, a shadowy bulk looming. He saw her. Too late to run. She turned toward him, ready to fight, to keep them away from her girl. A red rage obscured all thought. She lunged forward, raising the candlestick.

"Lane," he said.

It was Bertrand. Not a burglar. She lowered her arm. Her body sagged in relief.

He stepped into a pool of streetlight coming in the window and she saw the outline of his head, his familiar shoulders.

"Jesus, you scared me to death," she said. "I thought you were breaking in."

The adrenaline was still pumping through her. She forced herself to take a deep breath. She went to him, stepped into his embrace. She loved how their bodies fit together, loved to feel his breath in her hair. But he never came to her like this, in the middle of the night, never when Louise was home.

"You shouldn't be here," she said.

"I'm sorry," he said, "I know."

"Who were you talking to?"

"Come in the kitchen. I need your help."

He took the candlestick from her hand and set it down. She smelled his sharp metallic sweat, sensed his tension. Lane followed him in and switched on the overhead.

A boy stood beside the kitchen table, younger than Louise. He flinched at the sudden light. He was skinny, tall, with a recent haircut. He was dressed in basketball shorts and a T-shirt, its silk-screened logo obscured with reddish-brown stains. Dried blood flaked from his bare arms and legs. It was smeared across his forehead and one cheek where he must have rubbed his face. The boy stood there, trembling, looking at his puffy sneakers, expensive ones. One sock crusted in blood.

"This is Artie," Bertrand said. "My son."

Lane, astonished, stared at the boy. In all the years they'd been together, Lane had never met Bert's kids, had never wanted to. The boy's presence in her kitchen was a violation. She glanced around at the table piled with papers, the dishwasher door open, the calendar hanging on the wall by the phone, marked up with Louise's school events. Louise's physics textbook open on the counter next to Lane's sketches. Her eyes skittered back to the kid. He did not belong here. The light seemed to hit him differently.

"What is that," Lane said. "Is that blood?"

"It's not his," Bert said.

"Get him out of here," she said.

"Honey—" Bert said.

She turned and went back to her bedroom. Bert followed, still talking.

"This is an emergency, Lane. I wouldn't ask if it wasn't."

"Take him home."

"I can't. Look, I have to deal with some things. Can you just keep an eye on him, get him cleaned up, find him something to wear?"

"But his mother—" Lane began.

"Lane. I can't. His sister's having a slumber party. Our house is full of eleven-year-old girls."

Our house. His and his wife's.

"Whose blood is that?" she said.

"Please, Lane. I need you."

"Answer me. What the fuck is going on?"

"I'll explain when I can. Just get him in the shower. Bag up his clothes. His shoes, too. Keep him here till I get back, don't let him leave. Don't answer the door—"

"Who the fuck is coming to the door?"

"No one. Just in case. Keep him out of sight, okay? Keep him hidden."

"Louise is here."

"I'm sorry," he said.

"Jesus, Bert," she said.

"We'll talk later," he said. "I promise." He was already turning away.

"Do not leave," she said. "Do not leave him in my house. Bert."

"I'll be back as soon as I can."

She followed him to the kitchen. He put his hand on the boy's shoulder and spoke to him.

"Artie, she's going to help us. Do what she says. I'll be back. I'm going to take care of everything."

The kid nodded.

"Good boy," Bert said.

Lane and the boy watched him leave. The boy uttered a stifled cry when his father shut the door behind him.

"Goddammit, Bert," Lane said.

The kid looked at her for the first time. He resembled his mother, Lane noted. She'd seen plenty of pictures of her in the society pages.

"Be quiet," Lane said. "Come with me, the bathroom's this way. Don't make a sound."

She turned to go, but he didn't follow.

"Come on," Lane said.

He didn't move.

"Are you hurt?" she said, more gently.

He shook his head.

"What the hell happened to you?"

He opened his mouth, as though to speak, but let out a loud sob instead. Once he started he couldn't seem to stop.

"Hush," she said. "You have to be quiet."

But the kid was unable to control himself. His crying made Lane want to shake him.

"Forget it, don't think about it," she said.

She forced herself to reach out to him, and awkwardly patted his bloodied arm. "It's okay," she said. "Don't cry. You have to be quiet."

Gradually his sobs turned to loud hiccups, though his body still shook.

"That's better," Lane said. "Neither of us wants to be in this situation. Let's just get through it, alright? We'll get it over with. You are going to take a shower."

He nodded miserably and allowed her to guide him to the back bathroom. She showed him how to use the tricky old faucet, let the water run until it got hot.

"Get in," she said. "I'll go find you something to wear."

She left him there with the water running. She took a garbage bag from under the kitchen sink, then went to her bedroom to look through her clothes. The kid was skinny. He ought to be able to fit into something baggy. She found an old pair of paint-stained sweatpants and an oversize T-shirt. She knocked on the bathroom door. He didn't respond.

"Artie, I'm coming in, okay?"

She pushed the door open to find him standing there, still dressed, staring at his face in the mirror.

"Kid," she said. "Come on. Get undressed."

He was unresponsive, in shock or something. She'd never seen anything like it. She touched his shoulder, and he reacted—he gave a soft cry and his body crumpled inward. He moaned something unintelligible.

"What?" she said.

"I didn't mean to do it," he said, turning to her. His voice cracked, uneven and raw.

"Do what?" she said.

He shook his head.

"What did you do?"

"It was an accident."

"What was?"

He didn't answer. He shook his head like he was trying to dislodge some vision. He was trembling all over.

"Artie, don't think about it. Just get in the shower, alright?"

He made no move to get undressed.

"Kid, come on. We agreed, right? You have to get cleaned up."

He looked at her then.

"Who are you?" he said.

"Nobody," she said. "A friend of your dad's."

He looked, if possible, even more alarmed.

He was putting it together. He hadn't known. Bert should never have brought him here.

"I'm trying to help you," she said.

She shoved the clean clothes and the black garbage bag at him and he took them.

"Put everything of yours in this bag," she said.

"Don't—" His voice cracked again and he stopped.

"What?" she said.

"Don't leave me alone."

Jesus, she thought. She would never forgive Bert for this. The boy was going to break down again, start wailing at any second. He would wake up Louise, and everything would get much, much worse.

"Alright, I'll be right here, right outside the door. I can leave it open a crack, how's that?"

Artie nodded. "Thank you," he said.

"Get undressed."

She left the bathroom, pulled the door halfway shut behind her. She heard him undress and put his clothes in the bag, pull the shower curtain aside, step under the water.

"I'm still right here, Artie," she said.

Lane turned to see a figure standing at the other end of the hallway, watching her against the light of the open bathroom door.

"Louise," Lane said. "How long have you been there?"

2017

CHAPTER 1

Ava was on a train called the City of New Orleans, on her way to the actual city of New Orleans, where her grandmother lived. She carried a backpack filled with books and a small suitcase of clothes. It was summer. She had finished the eighth grade four weeks before. Her mother had been dead for three. Louise had walked into the emergency room with a bad headache, and twenty hours later she was gone. A freak thing, the doctors said—a rare virus that attacked the brain stem.

Ava watched the green landscape flip past her train windows. She tried reading Harry Potter but she was too distracted, so she paced up and down the train cars. She'd never been anywhere besides her home in Iowa and one trip to Chicago. The country seemed too big. Ridiculously big.

Her mother's roommate Kaitlyn had driven her to meet the train in Chicago. The three-hour trip from Iowa City had been laced with Kaitlyn's endless stories about her boyfriend, who may or may not have been flirting with his neighbor down the block, whom Kaitlyn described as "one of those overgrown Girls Gone Wild sluts, I mean, she's thirty years old for god's sake"; Kaitlyn's mother, who perpetually got on her nerves; and Kaitlyn and Louise's bitchy boss at the factory, who had been unexpectedly kind when Louise got sick. It was easy to be with Kaitlyn because she never stopped chattering and did not require a response. Ava knew she was doing it on purpose, keeping things light. They'd been crying for weeks and needed a break. Ava was tired and numb, relieved to be away from the pity on everyone's faces, and all the places where her mother should have been.

Kaitlyn parked in front of the train station in Chicago and handed Ava a sheaf of twenty-dollar bills.

"Keep it in your bra," she said.

The girl gave her a look. Kaitlyn was always being embarrassing.

"Or your sock."

"Thank you," Ava said.

"I wish I could come with you," Kaitlyn said.

"It's okay. I'll be fine."

"Don't let anybody talk to you."

"Okay."

"People aren't good, remember that."

She'd heard Kaitlyn say this before, it was one of her maxims.

"I know," Ava said.

"Smart girl."

Ava got out of the car. A printout of her train ticket was in her jeans pocket, creased and sweaty from her anxious hand. Her grandmother in New Orleans had paid for the ticket. Ava watched Kaitlyn drive off before she went into the station, found her platform, and boarded the train. She tried not to think about the speed at which it carried her away from home.

The train arrived in the afternoon. Ava had grown up hearing stories of New Orleans her whole life, and was half-surprised, now, to find that it was a real place. So far it was dirtier and uglier than she had pictured, the train station far less impressive than the ornate one she'd left in Chicago.

Ava looked around for her grandmother. She wondered if there would be a sign with her name on it, maybe some balloons or flowers like in the movies, when people arrived somewhere. She walked from one end of the station to another, scanning faces, more black faces in one place than she had ever seen before. No old ladies stood around waiting for her. She bought a Coke from a machine. She studied the mural that stretched above the ticket counter, a depiction, it said on the wall, of the history of New Orleans. The paintings were violent and disturbing, with dark colors and sharp angular figures doing terrible things to one another.

After a while she went outside and stood under the broad awning. A jumble of freeway overpasses loomed next to the building. The heat was shocking, thick. She waited there, trying to guess what kind of vehicle her grandmother might own. She imagined a plump gray-haired lady and a plush sedan, a jar of cookies, a guest room. She sweated against her backpack and her suitcase felt heavy and slick in her hand. She went back in to the air-conditioning.

Ava wandered around the station, past blue and brown chairs bolted to the floor. She found a pay phone and tried Lane's number but it rang and rang. Ava waited through a series of buses unloading, each dispensing a throng of people into the station. She checked outside again. No luck.

Back inside she was pacing, too anxious to sit. People around her surged toward and away from buses, hugged and stretched and dragged their luggage. Ava went for the third time into the gift shop and studied the souvenir trinkets and T-shirts. The lady behind the counter spoke to her.

"Hey, babe, can I help you find something in particular?"

"No," Ava said. "Thank you. I'm waiting for my ride." She stood next to a shelf of real baby alligator heads. They'd been coated in some kind of shellac and they glistened under the fluorescent fixtures.

"You been waiting a while. Maybe they're not coming."

Ava said, "I was thinking that, too."

"Where you trying to go?"

Ava opened her backpack and found the little book where she had written down her grandmother's address. She read it out.

"Dang, that's way Uptown."

"Could you tell me how to get there?"

"You could maybe take the streetcar, if it's running," the woman said.

"What's the streetcar?" Ava asked.

The woman frowned. "Maybe better if you have money for a cab. You have money?"

Ava nodded.

"Go see if there's one out there."

Ava thanked the clerk and walked into the humid heat and car exhaust of the Central Business District. She approached a waiting cab and gave the driver the address. He helped her with her case and she got in the car. A television played flashy celebrity gossip news in the backseat and Ava watched it as they bumped over rutted streets.

Ava had never been in a taxi before, but this experience was no less strange than any of the past three weeks. After the hospital and the funeral, the world was not what she had thought. Things happened and she observed them with a detachment that overlay a deep, unaccessed horror. Just get there, Ava thought. See what happens next.

CHAPTER 2

Lane hunched over the sketchbook on the table, drawing in a rush of focused energy, like the world might end at any minute. Nothing mattered but the work, even if it was some bullshit commissioned piece for a stupid hotel she would otherwise never set foot in. Something distressing lived in a part of her mind she had no access to, but she caught glimpses of it sometimes. Slivers of trouble coming, or trouble already happened and forgotten but spreading its damage around, just beyond the edges of thought.

The day was still, the light in the kitchen soft and diffused. Lane knew the paths of the sunlight in every room of the house. As a girl she had watched the angles of sun and shadow until she had them memorized. Fifty, sixty-something years ago. Now the house was like an extension of her intelligence, a container of memories she mostly ignored as she sketched.

This mural, for a new restaurant in the Marigny, was to be a landscape extending across four walls of the large dining room. A traditional scene of the neighborhood when it was still part plantation and a few narrow cobblestone streets. They wanted

authenticity, historical accuracy, photorealism—Lane's special-
ties. For weeks she'd been researching old maps and drawings.

She flipped through a book of costumes from the 1820s,
marking pages of French and Haitian dress styles. She lost herself in the details, studying and sketching, until her physical reality brought her back to the kitchen. Stiff muscles, hunger, a
headache that meant she needed caffeine. Crumbs on the table
from breakfast cast tiny shadows indicating late afternoon. She
stood and went to the refrigerator, poured a chicory coffee over
ice, and lit the pipe that had gone out in the ashtray.

Lane heard a knock at the door, then the bell. She put down
the pipe and went to answer. Caterers, the party, was that today?
She must have written it down somewhere, on a notepad, but
where was the notepad? She'd discovered in recent months that
things had a way of proceeding on their own, even if she forgot
all about them. People got alarmed when she asked questions
or acted surprised, so she tried to project an air of benevolent
nonchalance. She accepted whatever situation presented itself, as
though she'd been expecting it. The marijuana helped.

But it wasn't the caterers, just a neighborhood boy selling
buckets of popcorn for his soccer team. Lane sent him away
and set out her large transferware platters for the party, even
though it was her assistant Oliver's job. He would come over
and organize everything, and they'd have a cocktail before the
guests showed up. She depended on Oliver to see to all the small
irritating details of her life so she could concentrate on her art.
He'd worked for her for years now, since right after Katrina. She
smoked some more, took a yogurt from the fridge. She hated
having to eat. The dreary requirements of the body took up too
much time.

When she was young, she'd devoted so much of her days to
grocery shopping and cooking meals, trying out new recipes.

She used to bake her own bread, when her husband, Thomas, was alive. Absurd to think of it now. Lane rarely thought about Thomas anymore. It had been nearly forty years since he'd died—a flash flood, his car hydroplaned and hit a truck. Could have happened to anyone. There had been the baby to deal with, and the problem of making a living, raising the child. She'd got on with it, put the marriage behind her.

Lately thoughts of Thomas tumbled into the present, unbidden. They felt like visitations of some sort, a transporting of the past into the present. A memory took over, a complete sensory immersion, paralyzing: the smell of yeast; the ringing phone; flour motes dancing through a shaft of kitchen sunlight; the cramp in her neck as she held the receiver with her shoulder to keep her hands in the dough. Flour handprint on the receiver, flour on her dress and in her hair.

Lane listened to the voice on the line. *Ma'am, you need to come down here.* She hung up, watched the long cord curling around itself. Thinking only, the bread will be ruined and Thomas will complain. She would not have time to make more, what with the laundry, shopping, the other countless essential chores. But then she got ahold of herself. She covered the dough and put it in the icebox to stall the second rise, gathered up the baby, and drove to the hospital. When she got there she learned he was already dead.

She arrived home late that night, just her and little Louise. The dough had coated the outsides of the pans, having grown and bubbled up with yeast. The refrigerator was a mess, covered in dried dough. If she'd left right away, dropped the bread without a thought, and rushed to his side, maybe he would have lived. If she'd been more kindhearted, could she have seen him conscious once more? She could have been, one last time, the recipient of his gaze, full of love or disgust or whatever it was.

A month into young widowhood, she realized her days were less complicated than they had been before. Thomas had been too needy, like most men, unaware of the details that rendered their lives seamless, the cooking and cleaning and errands. Men were so helpless. They couldn't even feed themselves. The baby sucked away at her, too, sapping her energy and time, but you could hardly blame a baby.

Lane experienced a sense of relief, immediate and astounding, when she learned the accident had killed him. She loved him, she wasn't a monster. But that first wave of clarity, that sense that she would be fine, that a lot of things would be easier now—she'd been right about that. She moved through her days quietly, caring for the baby, all the while listening to the rising sound inside her, a buzzing voice that grew more insistent. Her life was starting. It was all hers. She would never have to give it up again.

Oliver let himself in, carrying a case of wine and a bag from the art supply store. He closed the door with his foot and set the box down on the sideboard in the dining room. Lane was sitting at the big mahogany table. He saw the platters piled up at one end.

"What the fuck's all this out for?" Oliver said.

Lane glanced up from her sketchbook. "What?" she said.

He pointed to the platters. She'd quit throwing her monthly parties two years ago now.

Lane shrugged. "Wanted to look at that pattern. For a sketch."

"Huh. Would have thought it was the wrong period. This is late 1800s, isn't it?"

"You think these restaurant idiots know that?" Lane said.

Oliver laughed. "They'll sue you if they find out."

He touched the edge of the Limoges. It was Edwardian

bone china, over a hundred years old, but the underside was chipped and the gilding mostly gone from the rim. Lane had run it through the dishwasher lord knows how many times, and it wasn't worth anything now. The house was crammed with used-up, ruined treasures.

"Well," Oliver said, "do you need it still?"

"No."

She lit the pipe and handed it to Oliver. She was running low, he'd have to get her more soon. He smoked and handed it back, but she was drawing again, a picture of an old wall telephone with a cord. Obviously not for the restaurant project. He wondered about it, but he had learned not to question Lane's process. She didn't think like ordinary people. You had to wait and see and then the end result was dazzling.

Oliver put the wine and art supplies away and carted the platters to the butler pantry, where they belonged. He could see she was engrossed, and it was his job to protect her from any distraction. He went through the mail, tidied here and there, made a note she needed milk. As he worked he listened for signs that she was finishing up. Then he'd fix them old-fashioneds, they could drink and talk. He'd make sure she ate something before he left for the night.

CHAPTER 3

Ava's cab parked in front of a wooden house, painted green. She paid and carried her bags to the front porch. The windows were leaded glass, wavy and old, distorting the reflection of the trees and telephone wires. Ava knocked.

After a minute a man opened the door. He was young, late twenties. "Yes?" he said abruptly, irritation in his voice. He held a drink in his hand. Beyond him in the fading light were high ceilings, crown molding, Oriental rugs.

"Hi," Ava said. "Is this where Lane lives?"

"Who are you?" he said.

"I'm Ava. I'm her granddaughter."

"Bullshit," he said. "What's this about?"

"Is she here?" Ava said.

"You got ID or something?"

She shook her head. "I'm only fourteen." Kaitlyn's warnings about strange men echoed through her head. "Who are you?" she added.

"Wait here," the man said.

He closed the door, leaving Ava on the porch. After a minute he came back and opened it again. "You better come in, I guess," he said.

She lugged her case over the threshold. A woman stood in the middle of the room—graying hair pulled back in a ponytail, a paint-stained dress. She looked old enough to be a grandmother, but unlike any grandmother Ava knew. The woman stared openly at Ava.

"Louise," the woman said.

"No," Ava said. "I'm Ava. Are you Lane?"

"Lane, what the hell is going on?" the man said.

"God, you look like your mother," the woman said.

"Really?" Louise had been beautiful, and Ava thought herself plain, awkward.

"Okay, god," the man said. "Let's go sit down. I'm Oliver, by the way. I could use another drink."

Ava followed them through a living room, dining room, and a dark hall to a kitchen at the back. Lane sat down at a wooden table. On it lay a spiral sketchbook, an empty glass, an ashtray and small wooden pipe.

"What'll it be?" he said to Ava. "Diet Coke, water?"

"Water, please."

Lane spoke. "I haven't seen you in ten, eleven years."

"I don't remember it," Ava said. "I was too little, I guess."

"Yes," Lane said. "You've grown."

It was nearly dark out, the kitchen in shadows. Oliver switched on the light. He poured Ava a glass from the tap and fixed drinks for Lane and himself, brought everything to the table.

"Louise is dead," the woman said. She was speaking as though she had forgotten and suddenly remembered a piece of trivia.

"Yes," Ava said.

"That your mom?" Oliver asked.

Ava nodded.

"Shit," he said.

He studied Lane's face, saw a quietness overtake her, like a scrim behind her eyes. He recognized that expression—she shut down sometimes, shut people out. She wasn't going to say much else.

"You eat?" he said to Ava.

"No," she said.

"Alright, I'll go pick something up. Give y'all some time."

Oliver left them, drove to the Rouses, and ordered red beans and rice, macaroni and cheese, and fried chicken at the deli counter. He picked up a tray of pecan bars and stood in line. Lane hadn't told him about this visit. Hell, he didn't even know she had a granddaughter.

Things slipped Lane's mind more and more frequently, but mostly they were of little consequence. Something this big—the daughter *died* and she hadn't told him? When had this visit been arranged? He paid for the food and drove back slowly through the neighborhood, taking the long route to avoid the worst potholes. He had a bad feeling about all of this, but he would do what he always did—clean up the mess. He would take care of Lane, whatever she needed.

Lane had finally quit staring at Ava. Instead she folded a paper napkin into smaller and smaller rectangles, creasing each fold sharply with a fingernail. Ava came around the table and bent down to hug the woman, but Lane stiffened before patting Ava uneasily on the shoulder.

"Sorry," Ava said. "Thank you for having me."

Lane nodded, studying the napkin, the table's surface.

"So this is where my mom grew up?" Ava said.

The question appeared to rouse Lane from her trance.

"Yeah," Lane said. "Not just her. I grew up here, too, and so did my father. His parents built this house."

"Wow, I didn't know that," Ava said.

She waited for Lane to respond, but her grandmother looked down at the table, said nothing.

After a minute, Ava said, "Is it okay if I look around?"

"Don't touch anything."

"I won't."

Ava left the kitchen, glad to get away from this strange woman. At the back of the house were two adjoining rooms. In the first, a wooden four-poster bed stood below a bank of windows. Lane's bedroom. Antique furniture, framed prints, paintings on canvas and postcards tacked around the walls. Everything in it seemed to belong there, even though nothing matched. The next room was utilitarian and messy, a work space. Shelves were loaded down with buckets of paint. Papers and books were stacked on every surface, and the air smelled of harsh chemicals.

Ava explored the rest of the house, the formal living and dining rooms, a large parlor with a fireplace, several bedrooms stacked with paint cans and art supplies, crates of drop cloths wedged between two old wardrobes. The place was cluttered, but most of the things in it looked old and expensive. She hadn't known her grandmother was rich. She tried to visualize her mother here and couldn't.

She crept down the dark hallway to a den with an old bulky TV on a cart in one corner, a sofa, a rug. French doors opened onto another room with shuttered windows on three sides, a kind of enclosed porch. Freestanding racks of clothes lined the space, and in the center was a twin bed, a bedside table, a lamp. She switched it on.

Clothing cocooned the bed, transformed it into a magical space lined with boas, long vintage gowns, assorted garments looped over hangers, yards of fabric. She examined the racks and found they were costumes—a Scooby-Doo outfit, a large foam rectangle that read SOAP with arm and leg holes. Wigs of varying colors and styles lay in a pile. A bright blue pageboy, a red Pippi Longstocking with braids wired to stick straight out.

She heard the front door open and close, then Oliver called out, "Dinner!" He and Lane were in the kitchen, spooning food from Styrofoam containers onto plates.

"Hey, come get some grub," Oliver said.

"Thank you," Ava said.

The red beans were good, almost like her mom's recipe, topped with hunks of grilled sausage. The three of them sat at the table. After a few bites a heavy lethargy overcame Ava and she pushed her plate away. She hadn't been able to eat much since her mother died.

"May I please be excused?" she said. "I think I need to lie down."

Oliver said, "Where are you gonna sleep? Lanie, do you have a plan?"

"No," Lane said. "Wherever, I guess."

"Can I sleep in the costume room?" Ava asked. "I saw a bed in there."

"Fine with me," Lane said.

"I'll check and see if it needs sheets," Oliver said. "Come on, let's get you squared away."

He pulled linens from a hall closet and Ava helped him make the bed.

"Alright, see ya," he said.

He closed the French doors behind him. Ava sat on the bed, imagining her mother as a girl in this same spot. The streetlight filtered in through the fabric, imprinting the room with an aura of protection. The heavy food, the heat and anxiety, her poor sleep on the train the night before, all these hit her at once and she lay back and slept among the costumes.

CHAPTER 4

In the morning Ava woke, her mind a blank until she underwent the daily torture of remembering. Grief had its own atmosphere that cascaded around Ava each morning. She recited to herself the litany of facts that had become her habit in the past weeks. Her place and circumstance, a retracing of steps. I am in the costume room at my grandmother's house in New Orleans. My mother is dead. I came by train. She recalled the backseat of the cab, the ride to Chicago with Kaitlyn, the funeral, the hospital. She'd been at a friend's birthday party when Kaitlyn called to say her mom was sick. She was surrounded by eight other girls, eating pizza and watching *Twilight*.

She heard sounds, water running, the scrape of a chair, and went toward them, her heart pounding audibly. She experienced a dread that she was used to, ever since the hospital. A feeling like wherever she was, it wasn't where she was supposed to be.

The sounds came from the kitchen. Lane sat at the table, drinking coffee and reading the paper. She looked up, smiling, but when she saw Ava her face froze.

"I thought you were Oliver," Lane said.

"Nope, it's me," Ava said. "Good morning."

"Well. Want coffee?"

"Yes, please," Ava said. Louise had never let her drink coffee, but sometimes Ava would sneak it. She and her friends used to walk to the Java House and buy lattes in secret. Lane poured a glug of cold brew in a glass over ice, added milk, and handed it to her.

"Are you hungry? There's probably something in there. Help yourself."

"Thanks," Ava said.

The pecan bars were on the counter from the night before. She put one on a plate and carried it to the table. She waited to see if her grandmother would reprimand her for having cookies for breakfast, but Lane didn't seem to notice. Oliver appeared in the doorway with a paper coffee cup.

"There you are," Lane said. "Everyone's crawling out of the woodwork."

"Good morning," Ava said.

Oliver grunted and poured his coffee into a mug. He leaned against the counter and took a long sip.

"Oliver's always like this in the morning," Lane said. "You have to let him warm up."

Oliver nodded to the girl. "I might have had too many mojitos last night. Possibly."

"Big night?" Lane said.

"John took me to this tiki bar in Central City. Super sketch. We couldn't sit outside because we heard gunshots. Nice drinks, though. Muddled cucumber and whatnot. Fresh herbs in everything."

Ava struggled to make sense of this speech. After a moment she said, "Who is John?"

"My boyfriend," Oliver said. "You got a problem with that?"

"No, of course not," Ava said.

"Good," he said. "Miss Nosy."

He set his coffee cup down and pulled a small wooden pipe and lighter from his pocket. He lit it, inhaled, and handed it to Lane, who did the same. Ava knew what it was, but she was astonished by how casual the adults were, smoking in front of her.

"Is marijuana legal here?" Ava said.

"Not technically," Oliver said.

"You're just like Louise, aren't you?" Lane said, inspecting the girl. She didn't sound pleased about it, Ava thought. The sugar from the cookie coated her teeth.

"So," Oliver said. He took another hit off the wooden pipe and spoke through his held breath. "I'm sorry about your mama. That's a tough one."

"Thank you," Ava said. That's how she had been responding when people said things like this.

"How long are you staying?" Oliver said.

"I don't know," Ava said. She glanced at Lane concentrating on the newspaper. "Do you live here?" Ava asked Oliver.

That got a laugh. "No, darlin'. I work here. You think I'd be this side of Canal if I wasn't getting paid for it?"

Ava had no idea what canal he was talking about. "Can I take a shower?" she said.

"Yeah, use that bathroom off the hall, there's towels in there."

"Thanks," Ava said.

The old lady was still sipping coffee as though Ava weren't even there. She went to take a shower, glad to be away from the two of them. What kind of people were they? Doing drugs right in front of her.

After the shower she dressed and found Lane and Oliver in the kitchen. They were still smoking, or smoking again, from the wooden pipe, and speaking in low tones when Ava entered. They stopped abruptly and looked at her.

Ava said, "Is it alright if I use your phone? I should tell my mom's friend I got here okay."

"What, are you out of minutes or something?" Oliver said.

"I don't have a phone," Ava said.

"Huh," Oliver said. "Where the hell did you come from, now?"

"Iowa City, Iowa."

Lane stood. "I've got to work," she said. "Oliver, can you—?"

"Yeah, yeah," he said. "We'll get out of your hair. Get some shoes on, Iowa. You're coming with me."

"Where?" Ava said.

"Errands. Come on." He was already leading her out of the kitchen.

In Oliver's car she pushed some trash aside with her foot. Go-cups, a free newspaper, a torn shirt on the floorboard.

"Is everything okay?" she said. "With my grandmother?"

"She works a lot. Try not to bother her, alright? She needs quiet."

Ava nodded, peered out the window at the city. The dusty thick glare, horns honking, people on the street, waiting in the heat for their buses. Brightly painted houses snugged right up to the sidewalks, dead palm fronds piled high in the gutters.

"But she forgot I was coming, didn't she?" Ava said.

Oliver shrugged. "She's not great with those kinds of things. But hey—you made it. Here you are." He smiled at her and turned into the Costco parking lot. "Got to pick up some stuff in here. But first things first. Let's go get you a phone. Never seen a kid without a phone before, it's too damn sad."

"You're buying me a phone?"

"Well. Lane's footing the bill, but yeah. Why don't you have one already? Are you like Amish or something?"

"No. My mom didn't believe in screens."

"What the fuck does that mean? Sorry. I got a dirty mouth."

"I don't mind," Ava said. "She read a lot of articles about child development and stuff. She said phones are bad for creativity."

"Well, you want one, or not?"

"Yeah, I begged her for one."

"Come on, then."

Inside the store, he helped Ava pick out a prepaid phone, then left her to choose a case while he went to get paper towels and groceries for Lane. He was happy to do a little something for the girl. She needed to cheer up or she was going to start getting on his nerves.

CHAPTER 5

In her heart Lane had always been a miserly person. When she was young she'd done her best to hide it, tried always to be the first on someone's doorstep with a pie if they got sick or had a baby. She was thoughtful, gave presents, volunteered. If a neighbor admired a scarf or some object of decor, she would insist the lady take it. In this way she kept a reputation as a kind, warm, generous woman. Someone you could count on.

But it was a deception. The outward scope of her generosity was in direct proportion to the rate at which her mind kept accounts. She couldn't forget any favor, no matter how small. She was always planning, calculating, charting out chores and errands she would need to do in order to make up for this gift or invitation and prepare for the next one. Her days stretched forward in small segments, in lists of ingredients. She knew exactly how many casseroles she could assemble while the pie crust rested in the refrigerator, exactly how many cups of raisins were in the pantry and could be used for scones at a moment's notice. Her head was full of lists, of quantities. She listened to herself sometimes, chatting with the other young moms, and wished she felt as relaxed as she sounded. She tried to turn off the constant tallying and the sense of growing resentment, but she couldn't do it.

It was a skill, that accounting, and it enabled her to make a living later on, when she put her business together. Trompe l'oeil murals, architectural painting. She had the talent, that had never been the problem. Thomas had been proud of her. He liked her creativity, but they both understood that her real job was taking care of him, their social engagements, the house, and the baby.

She managed it, even maintained an outward cheer that fooled Thomas and everyone else. He believed her to be as kind and giving and easygoing as she acted. For that reason she could never quite love him completely. Her daughter, on the other hand, saw right through every gesture of kindness. She didn't fall for any of it.

Once Lane had spent the day experimenting with a new pound cake recipe—she was a talented baker, good at anything that required precision. The cake had just come out of the oven when the lady down the block called to say her father was in the hospital and her children would be on their own, there were three of them and the oldest could babysit, but she wondered if Lane could check on them. If it wasn't too much trouble. Lane said yes, of course, and hung up the phone.

"I guess I'll take the cake over, once it's cool," Lane said to Louise.

Louise said, "Why, Mama? You spent the whole day on it. Now you won't know how it turned out."

"It's just a cake. They're having a horrible night. I can make another one for us."

"But you don't want to. You wanted that one."

Louise didn't care about the cake herself, she only liked cake with frosting. But she knew Lane was already calculating the hours lost, the next trip to the store—did she have enough sugar left, how long would it take to bring the eggs and butter to temperature? Louise understood that her mother viewed kindness as a trap.

Lane was afraid of Louise's ability to see her so clearly. Her love for her daughter was too enormous, she was helpless before it. She could do nothing about it, could not use it for anything. It was a useless mountain in the middle of her life. With her daughter, Lane never had the upper hand.

Louise left home at seventeen, and Lane had assumed it would be temporary. Their family had been in New Orleans for seven generations. The idea that her daughter might live somewhere else never occurred to her. If she'd been more on top of things, maybe she could have prevented it. Louise had always made her feel slow-witted.

In the last year of high school her daughter had become eerily gorgeous, and Lane could see she knew it. She'd found some boy from far away, a student at Tulane, and gone to wherever the hell he came from. Lane learned this later, in a note:

Mama, by the time you track me down I'll be eighteen anyways. I'm going to Iowa. Travis's family needs his help on the farm. Don't worry, I'm fine. xoxo Louise

It was the girl, Ava, putting these old thoughts in her head. Lane went back to her research, consulted a new book of architectural diagrams that Oliver had dropped off, but she couldn't concentrate. The dog up the street started to bark. Lane had got Louise a dog when she was seven years old, a pretty setter who howled at sirens. They named her Penelope. Now the dog was dead, and Louise, too.

The other dogs in the neighborhood started their chorus in response. Lane wished they would shut up. Wished she could shoot them. They weren't the type to have guns, her husband Thomas had said, they were civilized people, but Lane had one. It came from her uncle's house, along with a passel of antique linens and china, the old iron bed she slept in, and the mahogany chest in the living room. A pistol. Where was it? In a closet somewhere. In a dream inside a dream, that's how her memories were.

Lane put the book down and went in search of the gun. She could picture it in an old cigar box, wrapped in a handkerchief or a dinner napkin. Was it an image her brain had invented? She noticed that happening, visions that filled in logical gaps and turned out not to be true. She started in her bedroom closet, brought a step stool out and climbed on it, pulling down shoe boxes, hatboxes, piles of scarves, stacks of old paintings and letters. The house was too crowded. She should hire one of those organizing people to clear it. She smoked a bowl and gathered up the mass of scarves, none of which she'd ever wear. She carried them onto the sunporch and dumped them on the vanity.

The sunporch. The girl's room, now. Lane had to keep that straight. Maybe she ought to clear out some of these old Mardi Gras costumes, too. Make space, make her welcome.

Lane went back to her bedroom but it was in disarray, piles everywhere. She needed to lie down, her head was hurting. She cleared off a space, piling the old canvases and the boxes on the floor. Why was this stuff down from the closet anyway? She stretched out on the bed and closed her eyes, suddenly remembering where the gun was. She'd kept it in the side-board, ever since she started hearing about these break-ins in the neighborhood. Easy to get to in an emergency. Nonetheless the other image persisted: flowered cloth, cigar box, she drifted off.

CHAPTER 6

Back at Lane's, Ava and Oliver carried in the shopping bags. The house was silent.

"She's probably taking a nap," he said. "I'll see you later."

"Where are you going?" Ava asked.

"I do have a home, you know," he said.

They exchanged phone numbers and he bounded down the steps as though he couldn't wait to be free of her.

Ava crept through the house. Light flooded in the front windows, illuminating dust on the windowsills and tables. Ava found cleaning supplies in the butler's pantry and wiped down the surfaces. Her mother had insisted on keeping their apartment clean. Ava's actions were a reflex, but she also wanted to be on her best behavior so her grandmother would like her. They did not appear to be off to a great start.

Ava considered vacuuming, but was afraid it would wake Lane. She took her new phone to the costume room and sat on the bed. She'd been one of the only girls at her school without a phone. "Read," Louise said when Ava complained. "Make something. Let's do a project." They tried out complicated recipes.

They drew portraits of each other. They played the radio and practiced headstands.

Since Louise had died, Ava had done none of these things. She had watched hours of television each day, she had wandered on her own through Iowa City, picking purple flowers off the hostas along Court Street and eating their pollen. She hung around the library but was unable to read. She couldn't focus on anything. She walked to City High at night. Her friends' older siblings talked about high school play practice, their Spanish teachers, the pranks the seniors played, sneaking onto the grounds at night and loading the fountain with grapes. Once a group of kids brought a cow inside the school. The stories struck Ava as grown-up, exciting. She couldn't wait to start ninth grade. She supposed she would never go there now.

She called Kaitlyn's cell and left a voicemail saying she was safe at Lane's. Then she dialed the number of her best friend from eighth grade, Lucille. Ava had barely seen her since the funeral.

Lucille answered on the second ring, a breathless hello.

"Hey, it's Ava. I got a new phone."

"Ava, what's up, where are you?"

"I'm in New Orleans, at my grandmother's house. It's huge. It's like a mansion."

"Really? Does it have any secret passageways?"

Lucille got excited about stuff like that. The two girls had watched *Clue* on repeat the summer before, until they had the scenes memorized. They both loved the house in it, even if the movie was kind of old.

"I haven't found any, but I just got here. How's your summer going?"

"Good, I'm going to camp next week. Margaret and I hiked the creek today. We saw like five used condoms."

"Gross."

"Totally. We're about to go to the movies, but Margaret's mad cause she wants to go ice-skating at the mall. She has a new skirt that she thinks will go awesome with her skates."

"She's so obsessed with clothes."

"Maybe we'll do both. If she keeps whining about it."

Ava could hear Margaret singing some Beyoncé song in the background.

"We have to go," Lucille said. "When are you coming back?"

"I don't know, maybe not for a while. Have fun at camp."

"Yeah, have fun in New Orleans."

"Save my number, okay?

"Yeah, I will. Bye."

Ava ended the call, feeling more alone than before. Lucille used to not even like Margaret, but they hung out all the time now, ever since Ava's mom died. Ava didn't really know how to talk to her friends anymore. Her sadness freaked everyone out.

Ava called her own number in Iowa, though she knew no one would answer. She heard the familiar robot voice on the machine and was tempted to leave a message for her mother. But, of course, Kaitlyn would hear it and think she was crazy, so Ava hung up.

CHAPTER 7

Lane rose from her nap to early afternoon light. Her body felt heavy and weak. She needed to fix an iced coffee, smoke, and get back to her research. The restaurant owners wanted their family members depicted in the painting. They'd sent in photos last week that Lane hadn't even glanced at yet. There was so much to do.

What had woken her? Lane had vivid and disturbing dreams. They often left her disoriented, more drained than when she lay down to rest. Lane sighed and stretched, trying to rouse herself. As she shuffled down the long back hall she heard a noise. Perhaps she'd left the radio on? Though it didn't sound like the radio. She listened. A girl's voice.

Lane walked to the sideboard where she kept the pistol, took it out of the drawer. She'd heard about these neighborhood break-ins. Home invasions. The voice was coming from the enclosed porch above the carport. There was nothing in there to steal besides costumes, but she supposed burglars wouldn't know that.

The door was open. It sounded like the girl was on the phone. Is this what they did now, chatted casually with their friends, as if everyone's homes were their personal space? She almost laughed at the absurdity of it. Lane peeked around the doorway. A tall, skinny girl sat cross-legged on the bed. She was pale with dull brown hair, a nothing of a girl.

Lane pointed the gun in her direction and stepped into the room.

"Get out of my house," she said.

The girl stared, her mouth opened in shock.

Lane said, again, "Get out."

The girl seemed frozen, she didn't take her eyes off the gun. Then she smiled, or tried to.

"Lane, you startled me," she said. "Is that real? Is it part of a costume?"

Something was off, it was one of those confusing, dreamlike moments. This girl knew her name. Slowly Lane nodded.

"Yes," she said. "It's part of a costume." Lane tucked the gun in the pocket of her dress, the weight of it making the fabric sag. "I need some caffeine," she said.

The girl followed her to the kitchen. She was tentative. Lane had no patience for these timid, soft types of girls. This was one of those weak ones, Lane could tell. She hovered in the doorway while Lane fixed coffee.

"Is there anything to eat?" Ava asked.

"Look for yourself."

Lane didn't like being near the girl. She took her coffee and went to her studio. She opened her sketchbook and flipped the pages until she found what she hoped was there, an explanation of some sort.

> Phone call from Iowa—
> Kaitlyn—Louise's friend
> Louise is dead
> Ava visit June 3

Louise is dead. She read the words and watched her mind skip past them without comprehension. The girl was Ava, then. She checked the date on her phone. Today was the fourth, it added up. Lane reached in her pocket, something heavy tugged at the fabric. She pulled out the gun, turned it over in her hand. She must have meant to clean it. Well. She didn't have time for that now. She put it back in the sideboard.

She remembered the call, this young woman with the broad, flat accent, her daughter's friend. She'd asked the woman how old Ava would be now. Fourteen, Kaitlyn had said.

Lane thought of Louise at fourteen, frown-faced and disapproving. Louise would be thirty-seven this year. She'd been away longer than she ever lived here. Time was such a funny creature, the way it coiled, stopped, sped up, reversed. The only measure of it that had relevance to Lane was before, during, after a painting. She could see time in brushstrokes, in line, in an expanse of wall yet to be covered. Time was visual, it spread around doorways, over fields of plaster.

She turned to a clean page of her sketchbook, blessedly white and absent those three words, *Louise is dead*. She hadn't seen Louise since that Katrina fall, when she'd been working on a hotel ceiling in St. Louis.

She couldn't do those ceiling jobs anymore, on her back all day, on scaffolding. Time was in the body, too. But when Lane was painting, her body disappeared. She forgot to pee, forgot to eat. Forgot everything else. Occasionally she played music, but she forgot to hear it. Even sound fell away. The neighborhood noises and the hum of the refrigerator receded as Lane returned to her drawing.

She was paid top dollar because she put in the effort to get the details right. Her work was sharp and well executed, and for the last ten years she'd found herself with more job offers than she could take on. Brad Pitt and Angelina Jolie had hired her when they rebuilt their own house after the storm. She did a mural for their dining room.

After that she was featured in *Traditional Home* and *Martha Stewart* and *Southern Living*. She raised her rates and booked more interesting jobs. With the steady work, her painting improved. She was making significant money for the first time, and though she didn't need it—her father had left her plenty, along with the house, plus there was Thomas's life insurance—she felt powerful, accomplished.

But the travel wore on her. Too much anxiety about the details—when the flights left, how long to hold the mail, that sort of thing. She feared her home would be broken into while she was gone. She dreaded the travel itself—missed connections, delays, last-minute gate changes, running in the airport and still missing her plane, having to rebook a new flight and start all over, and CNN blaring from screens placed every twenty feet. She only worked in town these days. She was getting to be an old woman, she supposed.

She'd been lucky, though, in Katrina. She had a raised house on high ground. The basement took in water, but that's what it was there for. The damage was minimal, and she had been out of town, working in St. Louis. Like a lot of folks, she didn't talk about that year, didn't dwell on it. But New Orleans was different since then. It wasn't the old city she'd always loved. Used to be she knew every one of her neighbors, old families, folks still living where they'd grown up, like Lane.

She'd brought Oliver in to house-sit while she was away, and kept him on as her assistant after she quit traveling. She was too busy to deal with bills, the arrangements and errands that kept things running smoothly. She was happy to turn that over to someone else, and Oliver was detail oriented, diligent, funny when he wanted to be. He fetched books from the library for her research, brought in lunches, and remembered to brew cold-drip coffee when she was running low. He procured wine and marijuana, dealt with the lawn guy, and helped her keep the parties going.

She'd begun the parties—crawfish boils, live bands in the front room—a year after Thomas died. God, she had energy back then. Raising the girl, painting, keeping up with social obligations. She schmoozed with art people, fought to be included in group shows at galleries, she painted murals at cost to get her work seen, spent more than she made on supplies. Back then everything was a hustle.

The parties were a part of it, too. Reminding folks she was there, inviting important collectors and gallery owners, charming everyone. Her completed canvases prominently displayed above the bar, in the kitchen, throughout the house.

She did the powder room mural on a whim, and people raved about it. To give the small, windowless room a greater sense of space, Lane painted a flawless trompe l'oeil of swamp stretching into the distance, cypresses, shacks on stilts, ibises gleaming white as the porcelain fixtures. Everyone loved it, and she was hired to do private homes by the time Louise was in junior high.

At thirteen Louise had been a pill, constantly criticizing Lane. So Lane wasn't a great mother. Fine. She never claimed to be. Some things were more important than being at every goddamn PTA meeting and volleyball game. Lane was trying, but she had to do everything on her own, and she was busy. At least the girl did well in school, stayed out of trouble. They had their separate lives.

And then she was gone. Run north with some boy. Lane figured it was doomed as all young love and Louise would be back soon enough. With the house to herself Lane found she could relax, could concentrate better. She missed her daughter, worried about her, but everything was easier when she was on her own.

CHAPTER 8

Ava found some cold cuts in the refrigerator and a loaf of sliced bread.

As she assembled two sandwiches, with mayo and coarse mustard, she heard Lane go through to the dining room and open a drawer, then shuffle back to her studio. As soon as she had a chance, Ava would find the gun. Lane said it was fake but it looked real. She'd been around guns since she was little. Her dad, a farmer and hunter, had taught her gun safety, then taught her how to shoot rifles, shotguns, and his pistol. He had been a sweet, dutiful, modest man. A good father, before they lost the farm. Her mother said he couldn't live without the land, he died of a broken heart. But really, it was an accident. He'd been drinking, the gun went off. Their old neighbors found him in his truck, parked at the old place, facing the rows of last year's soy crop.

Ava brought the plates to the table and went to get Lane.

"Lunch is ready," Ava said. "I fixed you a sandwich."

Lane closed her sketchbook and carried it with her to the kitchen. They sat down to eat.

"Am I going to stay here?" Ava said. "Like, live here and go to school and everything?"

Lane studied the girl. "What about your father?"

"My mom didn't tell you?"

"What?"

"He died. Five years ago."

Lane absorbed this for a moment. She knew that. Of course she had known it. She'd simply had no reason to think about it before now. "His family?"

Ava shrugged. "They're all gone," she said. Her father, an only child, had inherited the farm when his parents died, before she was born.

"There's no one in, what is it? Iowa?"

"No."

"Well, we'll see," Lane said.

"What do kids around here do in the summer?" Ava asked.

The question caught Lane off guard. It was not something she'd considered before.

"I might be the wrong one to ask," Lane said. "Seeing as how I'm an old lady."

Then she smiled at Ava, and Ava saw her mother in the smile. Encouraged, Ava said, "At first I thought Oliver lived with you."

This made Lane laugh. "Oh, lordy. That's the last thing I need. I'm lucky to get rid of that boy at the end of the day."

He was definitely not a boy, he was probably as old as Kaitlyn, Ava thought. And he sure was drunk a lot. But he had known where to take her, what to do. Lane didn't seem to know anything.

"When does he come back?" Ava said.

"Monday," Lane said. "He'll bring in some materials for me, and some lunch. And he usually sticks around to deal with paperwork, financial things."

"Financial things?"

"He pays the bills, the taxes, does the checkbook."

"Why? I mean, why don't you do it?" Ava asked. Her mother paid her own bills and filed her own taxes. She had taught Ava how to be careful and smart about money. Ava had assumed all adults were this way.

"I'm too busy," Lane said. "Was never much of a math person anyway."

"I like math," Ava said.

"Your mother was good at math. She got straight A's all the way through."

"Yeah, I know," Ava said. A million questions welled in her. What was her mom like back then? Why didn't Lane ever come visit them? What was she carrying around that gun for? Instead, Ava pointed to the sketchbook on the table and said, "What's that?"

Lane showed her. As Ava flipped through the book, Lane explained her project. Some pages contained scribbled notes: dimensions, distances, lengths of doors and windows. Dollar amounts for time and materials, schedules, notes about lighting. Some pages had photographs taped in.

"That's the street outside the building," Lane said. "When they finish, that will be the view through the window. See this house? It was built in 1820, one of the first ones in the neighborhood."

Other materials were tucked in between the pages. Diagrams of old-fashioned garments, maps, carriages, horses, birds.

Ava was surprised to see how similar Lane's handwriting was to Louise's and her own. It gave her a momentary sense of comfort, followed by panging melancholy. Like her grandmother's smile, seeing the handwriting left her lonely and unsettled. Lane was still talking about the restaurant, her research, the history of the neighborhood that she had been studying. Ava turned another page and the sketches began.

"Oh," Ava said.

Her mother could draw, but not like this: both gestural and precise, with a freshness and energy that rendered the subjects more real than a photograph. The sketches were quick, unpolished, executed in ordinary pencil, often unfinished at one corner, their incompleteness the only thing that called attention to their artifice.

Ava had formed the impression that her grandmother was crazy and also perhaps a criminal of some sort. She was startled, now, to see that Lane was brilliant.

"They're amazing," Ava said. "I had no idea."

"She never talked about me, did she? I always suspected as much."

Ava kept turning pages, each graced with achingly lovely images: buildings, their minute architectural details suggested by a few rough lines. Figures. Women in long dresses and bonnets, men in old-fashioned suits, children and dogs and birds and trees. Ava had never seen anything like it.

Lane was explaining what the finished painting was going to look like, listing the details she still had to figure out. It struck Ava as an incredible extravagance that the sketches were for something else. They were perfect already. She turned a page and next to a half-finished rendering of a magnolia flower she saw the words. *Louise is dead.*

Lane stood over the sink rinsing plates when Ava closed the book.

"Done with that?" Lane said. "I've got to get to work. Try not to make too much noise."

"I won't," Ava said.

Lane took the sketchbook and her pipe back to her studio.

Ava dried their lunch dishes and stacked everything neatly on the shelves. The house was silent. Ava crept through to the dining room, opening drawers and cabinets. She found the gun in the large marble-topped buffet and picked it up. It was heavy, definitely real. She checked the chamber. Loaded. Why would anyone need a loaded gun in the middle of a city? It didn't make sense, what was there to shoot?

She carried it to the costume room, unloaded it, and hid the bullets and the pistol in separate pockets of a gingham dress with a frilly smock and bonnet—some sort of pioneer girl outfit. She wasn't crazy about hiding Lane's gun from her, but nobody should point a loaded gun at their granddaughter. Ava didn't want it to happen again. She hoped Lane wouldn't get mad.

Afraid to bother her grandmother, Ava went outside. She walked past old houses, their windows of rippling glass, air-conditioning units humming in the side yards. Messy banana trees and crape myrtles dominated the small lots, overflowing their fences. It was lush and green like Iowa in late summer, but this vegetation was unfamiliar to her.

She came upon a park a couple of blocks away. A paved trail circled the park's perimeter, congested by dog walkers, people exercising, an old man shuffling along with a cigar. She crossed the path and walked on the grass, past families with small children, toddlers chasing ducks along a lake. Overhead huge oak tree branches met and formed a canopy, their roots bucking out of the ground. Ava wandered along, staying in the shade of the large trees. Even here she noticed garbage everywhere. Take-out containers, empty beer cans and cigarette butts.

Some peewee soccer teams were practicing in the fields, and a family gathered around a grill, cooking some meat. Nearby a girl of eight or nine sat erect on top of a horse. Ava kicked her way along the sidewalk above the cypress trees growing out of the water, until they thinned out and she could see the other bank, the cranes and barges across the waterway. The Mississippi formed the eastern edge of Iowa, they'd been there on a field trip last year, to Dubuque, where they'd learned about the old industrialists who'd built their mansions above the river, at the top of the bluff. It seemed impossible that anything from that place could touch this one.

She turned away from the bank and walked back through a different part of the park. She came upon a broad green space that had the biggest tree she'd ever seen. It must have been hundreds of years old. Some of its branches rested on the ground. Its gnarled roots twisted out of the earth as high as her waist. Ava climbed up one of the roots and rested against the trunk. In the distance, runners bounced past in their neon gear, and beyond that, cars on the street, their reflective surfaces glaring.

The tree's massive canopy created its own sense of space, a different energy, detached from the pace of the street. Ava breathed it in. Her mother might have come to this tree. She could have sat in this exact spot when she was Ava's age. For the first time Ava found it possible to imagine her mother in the city. She stayed in the park for the rest of the afternoon.

CHAPTER 9

Artie ran five miles every morning. He loved to be out before the sun was up, to come awake in the dewy streets along with his city, to feel his legs working, his heart pumping efficiently. In his head, he revised the speech for his first campaign event. He'd be officially announcing his candidacy in a week. Yesterday at the new office they'd unfurled his banner, fresh from the printer.

ART GUIDRY FOR CITY COUNCIL AT-LARGE.
ART IS RIGHT FOR NEW ORLEANS.

He'd gotten choked up when he saw it. He wished his dad could have been there. The future they'd planned for so long was finally happening.

The announcement party would be a crawfish boil in the park. He envisioned himself smiling at the gathered crowd. *His* crowd. They'd invited Artie's old school friends who were lawyers and judges and real estate developers now, his mother's Junior League contacts and his dad's old colleagues and supporters. His father, Bertrand Guidry, had spent decades on the city council, and his machine would get behind Artie. He hadn't seen a lot of those folks since his dad's funeral. Two years ago, already, but the pain of that loss was hardly diminished. Now that he was entering politics himself, he longed for his father's advice.

Art knew he'd win. He had the name going for him—his father had been widely adored, and everybody was in favor of a Guidry on the council again. He had the talent, and more important, he really believed the things he said, about education, cleaning up corruption. New Orleans deserved better. Deserved someone like him, who loved this city, wanted to help, and had the energy to take it on.

And this was only the beginning. He wouldn't stagnate in the city council like his dad. He had ambition. He'd seen the world beyond New Orleans, understood how it worked. He'd be in D.C. one day, on the Senate floor. Sometimes in the solitude of his early morning runs, he let himself imagine it.

Toward the end of his route through City Park, he passed a playpen of puppies set up in the grass. He doubled back to check them out. The girls had been begging Artie and his wife, Marisol, to get a dog for at least a year, but it hadn't been feasible with the new house, the renovation, and little Pearl still in diapers.

"See if you still want one when you're five," he'd told his older daughter, Colette.

"Daddy, I will want one when I'm five one hundred," she had said, her little face grave.

"I think she means it," Marisol said.

Colette's fifth birthday was approaching and she still talked about a dog nearly every day. Pearl was potty-trained now, hadn't had an accident in weeks. And they were finally in the house, a double shotgun in the Garden District with the new kitchen and family room they'd added on. Maybe it was the right time for a pet.

Three college-aged kids in turquoise T-shirts sat at a table next to the dogs. They had a stack of brochures. One of the young women came forward.

"They're cute, aren't they?" she said. "Want one?"

"What's this?" Artie said.

"We're from New Beginnings." She pointed to the logo on her shirt. "We're a no-kill shelter. Here, hold one. This guy's my favorite."

She handed him a squirmy fat-bellied brown animal the size of his forearm. The puppy wiggled and licked, his little paws kicking out in all directions. Artie laughed, loved him immediately. He gazed into the puppy's hazel eyes. "Hi, little buddy, what's your name?"

"We've been calling him Boudin," the woman said. "But, obviously, you can change it, he's young enough. We found him and the rest of his litter in a box by the Fairgrounds. They've already had their first round of shots."

"He's cute," Artie said. "But I think I better check with my wife."

"You could surprise her," the girl suggested.

Artie laughed. "I can see you're not married," he said.

"Nope, I'm single, actually." She twisted a lock of her hair and smiled at him.

Jesus, Artie thought. He hadn't meant to flirt. But women liked him, always had. Men, too. Everyone did.

He handed the puppy back and shook her hand.

"Art Guidry," he said. "I'm running for city council this November. I appreciate the work y'all are doing. I'll talk to my wife about it. Can I get a brochure?"

"Sure." She gave him one and made the little puppy's paw wave goodbye.

As he continued his run, an idea began to form. He could use this. There'd been a recent scandal with the public animal

shelter—a series of resignations following corruption allega-
tions. The board was accused of siphoning money and shelter
resources to private companies, hiring so-called consulting firms
with public funds, and, worst of all, excessive euthanasia. He'd
followed the story, horrified. A spate of no-kill adoption orga-
nizations had emerged to try to help the displaced animals.

Artie would have to do some research, make sure whatever
shelter he dealt with was on the up-and-up. This would be a
great visual for the anticorruption message in his platform. An
actual puppy, his daughters' little arms around it—PR gold.
Boudin wasn't a bad name, either. Clever, local. They could do
a video interview, get still photos for the billboards. He'd talk
to Marisol and Albertine, his campaign manager, and set it up.

CHAPTER 10

By the end of the first week Ava realized that Lane did not care where she went or how long she was gone. In fact, Lane paid her little notice. When they encountered one another in the house, Lane always seemed baffled by Ava's presence.

Oliver came over most days. Sometimes he consented to Ava's company on his errands—trips to the library at Tulane, lunch runs to an astounding variety of sandwich shops and seafood places, burger joints, Thai cafés, Middle Eastern and African and Vietnamese delis, and greasy corner restaurants with interchangeable menus of gumbo, red beans, étouffée, oyster loaves, iceberg lettuce salads.

Oliver drove her one day to a little bike shack in Riverbend, on the other side of the park. He told Ava to choose a bike from the dozens the guy had stashed in his shed. Oliver paid cash for it and let her ride it home, after quizzing her about the directions. "Can't have you getting lost," he said.

After that Ava occupied herself by exploring. Despite Oliver's edict, she got lost every day, but by finding her way back, she began to learn her way around. The geography of the city perplexed her. It seemed to her as though the New Orleans streets had spilled out of a can from a great height, and just stayed where they landed, overlapping in nonsensical angles. The entire state of Iowa was laid out in a grid. Everything made more sense there.

She sweated her way through the streets. Plastic beads hung in the branches of trees and on telephone wires. Garbage lay everywhere—plastic cups and broken flip-flops and crumpled newspapers strewn over the sidewalks and in the gutters. She noticed a lot of graffiti, elaborate spray-painted tags on the sides of buildings and the backs of billboards. She decided to go to the French Quarter, because she knew it was famous. She followed the river there. The streets smelled like beer, even in the morning. She walked her bike up an alley, past Dumpsters and doorways of crumbling brick. It opened onto a broad square where a man propped paintings against an iron fence. Depictions of the same fence appeared in many of the paintings, acrylics on canvas board. Ava could tell they weren't very good. The repeated iterations of the fence, the street musicians who sang songs about singing songs in New Orleans—Ava felt lost in this strange place so enamored with itself.

She thought of the old farm. One particular October day of intense blue she and her dad watched an orange fox and her kits file along the road and duck into a tunnel of high grass. The colors were impossibly bright. Back then, when both her parents were alive, she used to think bad things came in from the outside, poaching from the edges of the field. Now she understood that even the house, the barns and sheds, the prairie fire crabapples and the oozing maples were made of death. Annihilation was right at the center of life, ready to erupt and cover everything over with loss. She was nine years old when her father died, they lost the farm, and moved to town. Iowa City had been overwhelming to Ava back then, but she saw now how tiny and sparse it was compared to New Orleans.

She liked to ride along the levee at the lake, for the sense of space it gave her. She returned to the Quarter to roam through the market and the small side streets. She listened to the musicians and shyly put coins in their cases. She set arbitrary goals for her day. Once she tried to find Lane's restaurant where the mural would be, but she got lost and ended up in Mid-City.

Ava came in one day from a bike ride and found every surface of the kitchen covered with dismantled shelves and drawers and condiments from the fridge.

Oliver was cleaning out the refrigerator. He had the TV going on the counter, tuned to some reality show of people fighting. It created a nice homey background noise.

"Just in time, Little Bit," he said. He handed her a vegetable bin filled with warm soapy water. "Carry this to the fridge and find yourself a rag. We need to wipe down everything in there, it's disgusting."

"What if I had plans?" Ava said.

"You don't."

It was true, she had nothing else to do. Oliver carried the trash outside, brought Ava some clean rags. The TV droned on. Ava's mother had hated these kinds of shows, people's private lives out in the open, showing off their worst selves. Ava listened, fascinated. A young couple was in a dispute about their child, accusing each other of bad parenting, infidelity, neglect, failures emotional and financial. Lane was drawing in her studio, so they kept the volume low. Oliver scrubbed and dried the shelves.

"That's more like it," he said, inspecting the inside of the refrigerator. "This really needed doing."

"Yeah, it was pretty gross," Ava said.

The show ended and commercials came on, then the news. Ava half-listened to the unfamiliar local ads, the newscasters and the weather lady who were strangers to her. She longed to hear the familiar jingles of midwestern hardware stores and the used-car dealers of Iowa City and Coralville, the voices she'd grown up with. These foreign commercials, the ads anyone would tune out, reminded Ava how far she was from home.

Lane shuffled in, her eyes vague, as though she was concentrating hard on some faraway problem. She reached to open the refrigerator and halted, as if jarred awake by the already open door, Ava kneeling before it. Lane blinked and stepped back.

"What the hell?" she said. "Where's the coffee?"

"I gotcha," Oliver said. He retrieved the carafe from a cooler near the sink and found her a glass. "Coming right up."

"Put everything back where it came from, alright?" Lane said.

"Naw, we're rearranging, just to mess with you," Oliver said.

Ava glanced up, uneasy. She had never tried to tease Lane and wondered how she'd take it. Ava was stunned to see Lane's face soften to a near-smile.

"Got to keep you on your toes," Oliver said. "Here." He handed her the coffee, darker than Lane usually liked it, but she drank and did not complain.

"Smoke break?" Oliver said.

"Why not?"

They watched Ava clean as they passed the wooden pipe back and forth. The smell of marijuana wafted around Ava. She was beginning to like it, to associate it with sunny mornings in the kitchen. The television was running political ads for the upcoming election. Lane shushed Oliver, who was asking about the order at the art supply store. She peered at the TV.

"I don't believe it," she said. "This asshole. I don't believe it."

"Who?" Oliver asked.

She pointed to the man on the television. He was delivering some rehearsed lines about updating traditions and serving his city. The tiny screen showed the man putting his arm across his wife's shoulders as she and a couple of little kids joined him in the shot. The four of them smiled at the camera and an off-screen voice said "Art Guidry for City Council at-Large. Artie is right for New Orleans."

"That little shit," Lane said, shaking her head. "Can't believe he came back."

"Who, him?" To Oliver, he was the same as the rest: rich guy in a fancy suit, lying to get votes.

"He's got some nerve. When I saw him last he was crying his eyes out, covered in blood."

"Covered in blood?" Ava turned to stare at Lane. This was way weirder than the things she usually muttered about. Her voice shook, too.

"Lanie? You alright?" Oliver said. "Here, sit down."

"He takes after his mother," Lane said. "He should never have come back."

She was still staring at the TV, even though the picture had changed and a new show was starting.

"Lane, you're pale," Oliver said. "Ava, let's eat lunch, come on. There's sandwiches in the cooler."

Ava brought the food to the kitchen table where Oliver had managed to get Lane to sit. "Eat," he said. "Maybe you smoked too much on an empty stomach. Ava, did she eat dinner last night?"

"I'm not sure," Ava said.

Oliver gave her a look. "Get her a glass of water."

"I'm fine, quit this fuss," Lane said. But she took a bite of the sandwich.

"Mustard?" She frowned at the po-boy.

"That one's mine, sorry," Oliver said. "Now you owe me a bite."

The people on the show were laughing. Oliver gave her the other sandwich and muted the TV.

"Drink your water, too," he said, watching Lane chew and swallow. Her color was coming back.

"Quit staring at me. I'm fine," she said. "Seriously, stop it."

"Sorry. Okay. Ava, how's that fridge? Let's finish it up."

They reassembled the clean shelves and drawers in the refrigerator and transferred the food from the cooler. Before they were done Lane went back to her studio, left her sandwich on the table.

"Nice job here," he said, appraising the clean refrigerator. "Let's try and keep it this way, alright?"

"I'm not the one who spills stuff," Ava said.

"Okay, Miss Perfect. You hungry? I got you a sandwich, too."

"Thanks," Ava said. "Does she really know that guy? What was she talking about?"

"I don't know," he said. "But do me a favor, will you. Don't ask her about it. You saw how upset she got."

"Okay. But what did she mean, covered in blood?"

Oliver shrugged, tidying the counters. He wrung out the wet rags in the sink. "She says all kinds of crazy shit. Haven't you noticed? That's just Lane."

"It's weird, though, right?"

"Not my job to try and figure out every cryptic thing that comes out of her mouth. That would be a full-time gig. I got enough to do already. I'm starting some laundry, do you have anything?"

"I can do my own," Ava said.

"Well, go get the towels then, and bring them downstairs."

Ava gathered towels and took them down the treacherous

basement steps. Light from above sifted through gaps in the floorboards. The ceiling was low and the basement dim. Dried mud covered the floor in places. She started the load, hoping Oliver would stick around to put clothes into the dryer. She didn't like it down there.

Upstairs she called Kaitlyn.

"What's happening, roomie?" Kaitlyn said. "I miss you!"

Ava laughed. Kaitlyn hadn't called her that since Ava was twelve and Kaitlyn moved into the spare room. It had been a novelty, at first, like having a friend stay over on a school night. Kaitlyn lightened the mood at their place. She was silly, loud, messy. Those years after Ava's father died had been sad and hard. With Kaitlyn, Louise laughed sometimes. Their lives were less orderly. Ava liked it.

"I miss you, too," Ava said. "It's kind of weird here."

"I was there on spring break once," Kaitlyn said. "I barely remember a thing. Partied too much. I'm sure I had fun, though."

"There's a lot of that," Ava said. "People drink like crazy. I miss Iowa."

"Oh, nothing's going on here. I mean, not a darn thing. Same old same olds. Starting to see those Early Girl tomatoes at the market. Remember how excited your mom would get about stuff like that?"

"Yeah," Ava said. It was true, Louise loved how you could grow food so easily in the Iowa soil. She got infatuated with the ripe melons and tomatoes, devoted her spare time to making pies when berries were in season.

"So what's your grandmother like?" Kaitlyn said.

"Um," Ava said, "she's okay. Kind of hard to talk to. She's pretty busy. She's a really amazing artist, though."

"I think I heard about that, yeah. That sounds cool."

"And she has a personal assistant."

"Assistant? Like some girl who picks up dry cleaning? My friend Shelley has a job like that in Chicago."

"No, it's a guy. His name is Oliver."

"A guy?" Kaitlyn's voice changed. "Does he live there, too?"

"No, but he's here a lot."

"I'm not too crazy about that," Kaitlyn said.

"Kaitlyn, chill. He's gay."

"Oh. Well, that's okay then."

"God, you always think everyone's a child molester."

"That's cause people are," Kaitlyn said. "You have to be careful."

"I am. Jeez."

"You're a smart girl."

Ava had already decided not to mention the pistol or the marijuana or Lane's memory problems.

"It's fine here, really," Ava said. "I promise."

"Okay. Good. Love you, girl."

"I love you, too," Ava said. It felt nice to say it to someone.

Ava wondered how things might have been different had her mother known she was going to die. You should've told me about Lane, Ava thought. At least I could have known what she was like. Could have been more prepared. Now here they were, living together, and Ava had no idea how to handle it.

She resolved, before the next phone call, to come up with some good things to tell Kaitlyn.

CHAPTER 11

Since the girl came, Lane felt the pressure Ava exerted, her quiet, pleading need and her concern. It radiated from the costume room, came in swells from wherever the girl was. How could anyone get work done? Lane went for a drive, she had to get away, the girl's sorrow saturated the house. What a joke for them both, to be shoved together. She pitied the child, but what could Lane do? They were strangers to each other, Louise had seen to that.

Anger flared in Lane's chest. At Louise for leaving, Louise for judging, for keeping herself apart. Didn't she realize Lane would need her one day? Louise, Miss Know-It-All, had managed to overlook this possibility. She stayed away, kept to herself, and then died. Lane didn't even have a clue where her daughter was buried, no one had told her. They probably set her straight in the ground, where she would rot and turn to dirt. It wasn't right. She ought to be here, in the family crypt. Housed.

Lane turned onto North Rampart, parked in the pay lot, and crossed the street to the entrance of St. Louis Cemetery Number One. A tour group filed past the guard at the gate sweating under his umbrella, and Lane joined them at the rear. She had brought with her a bouquet of broad leaves from the elephant ear begonia growing in the backyard. It was plain, tropical. She could have bought flowers somewhere, but these leaves seemed more fitting. About twenty years ago Bert had suggested to her that she let the elephant ear take over, instead of fighting it to make room for her bulbs. She'd quit planting, she'd let the beds get overgrown. She liked the way the leaves slid against one another in the breeze, a smooth rustle, like friendly companions speaking in a hush.

Bert knew her better than anyone, that was the thing. He knew what she needed and he gave it to her. Or gave her permission to take it for herself. Bertrand's own yard won those neighborhood awards. His wife amended the soil to turn her hydrangeas unnatural colors, she clipped her hedges, planted her beds with hundreds of purple pansies. Lane had cruised by once or twice—she wasn't above that, necessarily. Roses, lupines, azaleas, always something flowering.

Lane had not attended Bertrand's funeral. She wasn't interested in any kind of scandal, had no desire to see his widow, his family, his colleagues. They'd go on and on about his legacy as a city councilman, his service to his community. None of that mattered to her.

She waited until the next day to go to the cemetery, to press her hand to the wall of the crypt sealed with his body inside. She'd had to bribe the guard to let her in, since she hadn't called ahead, did not have permission from the archdiocese. Why would you want to be buried in a place like that? She'd always hated this cemetery, here on the edge of the Quarter. Cracked and broken, nothing but plastered brick and narrow aisles and centuries of sadness. No trees, no green anywhere except stifled little ferns growing horizontally out of cracks in the tomb walls.

Tourists crowded against the tombs to stay in the shade, sweating while the tour guide fast-talked about Marie Laveau.

Lane hated the things people said about death and loss. The clichés did not come close to describing the bleak depth of it, the loneliness that never, ever ends. If it weren't for Oliver she might have let herself starve. She owed that to him, keeping her going, but she couldn't help but resent him for it, too. The only thing left to her when she emerged from that acute phase of grief was her painting, and she shoved herself into it like logs in a fire. Fine with her if she didn't make it out.

Lane recognized she wasn't the same as before. Her mind had aged, it forgot things. Maybe she had a brain tumor or something. The world felt more and more like a hostile place full of malevolent strangers. Bertrand had known her and loved her. Both those things together were so unlikely to coincide. Now Louise was gone, too.

A couple of goth teens skulked past the tombs on the next path. Lane eyed their fishnet tights worn under cutoff shorts, their band T-shirts and black boots. One carried a camera, an old Pentax. Any photos they took would end up overexposed, too much contrast in this harsh light. Lane propped her bouquet on the side of Bertrand's tomb. She was glad her family crypt was in a smaller cemetery, with old trees and fewer tourists. She passed another tour group on her way out, a gaggle of sweaty miserable people in ugly sneakers huddled together in the shade. She entered the Quarter and stepped into a bar, ordered a fruity rum cocktail in a plastic cup. She needed the sugar; she'd been prone to light-headedness lately.

As she walked back to the car, she sipped the drink, resentful of her aging body. Lane hated any weakness in herself. She tossed the cup in a can at the parking lot's entrance. In the car she turned on the air and let it run for a bit, cooling off. She drank from a water bottle, hot and tasting of plastic. Her body, the things it needed—food, water, rest—had always been an inconvenience, but lately it was worse than ever. She shouldn't have come out in the heat of the day, she sensed a headache coming on.

Lane was prone to migraines, especially when there was weather moving up from the Gulf. She drove home and closed her curtains on the shifting pressure and gray light of the impending thunderstorm, trying to breathe into the pain, trying to sleep. She drugged herself with coffee, aspirin, marijuana, ice packs on the back of her neck. She tried to treat the headache as a meditation, to inhabit it and accept it.

She hadn't caught this one early enough, deceived by the euphoria that preceded the pain. She'd awakened that morning feeling like she was floating through the house, distant from the dishes, the balls of dust along the floorboards, the trim that needed repainting. She saw everything from a slightly new perspective, and she didn't care about any of it. The not-caring was a profound solace, a delight. A dose of Excedrin would prevent the headache but it would knock out the euphoria, and in that altered state it was hard to recognize the aura for what it was.

She didn't have to ask Ava for silence. The girl appeared to know by reflex to leave Lane alone. Lane heard her whispering to Oliver and then the sounds ceased. Her vision blurred but her hearing in this state was unbearably sharp.

At the sound of the telephone Lane nearly wept. It rang twice, each sound taking up space behind her eyes and lingering there, surging into the throb. The two rings pulsed, overlapping each other, even after the sound had ended. When the ringing began again she thought: Bertrand. It was their old code: ring twice, hang up, call back. She heard Louise answer and resigned herself to whatever might happen next.

"Hello," Louise said—whispered, to protect Lane who had one of her headaches. Louise understood how sound pierced walls and split her mother's mind into pieces.

"Hello?" Louise said again, but he would have hung up—he knew better than to talk to Louise.

Some amount of time passed. It was dark out, from night or the storm, Lane couldn't tell. She started to feel better when the rain finally started. The phone again: two rings, a pause, then ringing. Lane answered, spoke to Bertrand, told him to come.

The rain on the windows continued, hypnotic and loud. Lane waited until Louise had gone to bed, then got up to wait for him in the kitchen.

In his late forties, Bert was still strong and fit. His graying temples suited him, and he'd always worn his clothes well, especially now that he had money to spend. He wore a handsome suit, collar unbuttoned, tie rolled up in his pocket. He left his umbrella on the kitchen balcony and removed his shoes when he entered. The path from the back alley and the steps up to the kitchen she kept maintained just for him, for privacy. He worried about his car being recognized on the street.

He kissed her hello on the corner of her mouth. Lane was glad to see Bert, though she wasn't at her best. She'd smoked too much, which finally put her headache to rest but left her hazy, unable to think. She regretted the lost hours of work.

"Who was that, this morning, who answered the phone?" he asked.

"The kid, who else," she said.

"She sounded so grown-up," he said. "Does she know anything, do you think?"

Lane shrugged. "Could be. She's smart. She doesn't speak to me."

Bertrand frowned but changed the subject. "You don't look well," he said. "Did you eat today?"

Lane shook her head. "Headache," she said.

"It's gone now?"

"More or less."

"Sit down, I'll fix you something."

She took a seat at the table and watched him move around her kitchen, comfortable in her space.

Their agreement suited Lane. He did not come by unannounced. He did not discuss his wife or children. She spoke of him to no one. They'd started as lovers, before either of them had married. When he met his wife, Lane was glad that some other woman would shoulder the burden of his official public persona. His place on the council, his social engagements, his children at the best schools. Marriage hadn't agreed with Lane, though she'd been faithful to Thomas while he was alive. Once he was gone, she saw no reason not to pick back up with Bert. She had missed him. She was grateful to be loved by him and not have to take care of him. It bothered her that he loved his wife, too, but she would not have traded places with that woman, even if it meant giving him up.

Lane needed her own space, time alone, independence. She liked privacy, she liked secrets. Lane could not offer constancy, support, dinner on the table. Taking care of a child was bad enough, but a man, too? Their love would have shrunk under the strain.

She found the secret exciting when they were young. The intrigue, the sense they were getting away with something. The risks they took, the anxiety that they might be discovered.

The prospect of that ruin endowed their meetings with romance, a delirium it may not have otherwise had.

These days Lane valued the secrecy, but for the opposite reason: it made her feel safe. She did not have to compromise or explain or suffer awkward encounters. She could take other lovers, if she chose, though it had been years since she'd bothered with anything like that. She had no interest in other men, or in most people. There was Louise, and Bert, and her painting, and she liked to keep them separate.

She picked at the omelet he set before her.

"Sorry, love. I wish I was more with it today," she said.

"You're alright, just eat. This weather always gets to you."

He brought her a glass of water. The food tasted like sand, but she swallowed a few bites. After the meal they talked about his job. He was trying to push an ordinance through the city council, a school funding bill that could affect the primacy of charter schools, but he wasn't making any headway. Bert cared about public service, and he understood the corruption that made everything run. The network of favors and manipulations suited him. He had that kind of mind.

He risked plenty, coming to her. He trusted her, he gave her so much power. She could destroy his family and his career with a single phone call. She could probably send him to jail with what she knew. Lane wondered how often he considered that. Sometimes she thought the potential for destruction was a measure of his love.

He tucked her into bed, turned off the light, and left the way he'd come, through the kitchen and down the balcony steps, to his car in the alley. *He still takes the risk, I still keep his secrets,* she thought. The more successful he was as a public figure, the more years of marriage, the children—each year he had more to lose, and yet he kept coming to her. He never questioned her loyalty, not that she could tell. She thought for the millionth time how absurd men were. How needy and stupid. On the other hand, he was right. She'd never, ever betray him.

CHAPTER 12

1997

Artie, Bertrand's oldest boy, possessed an amount of charisma rare even among his family members. Everyone loved him. It had been this way for as long as he could remember. He had stood bewildered in the center of a preschool classroom as the other toddlers knocked one another down and cried, competing to be near him.

He experienced the burden of leadership before he understood what it meant. He felt a responsibility to live up to the admiration of his classmates and his teachers. Artie tried instinctively to limit his capacity to harm. He was nice to everyone, he learned to tell jokes, to entertain, to earn the admiration he received. He was a sweet boy, an honor roll student. He tried not to offend anyone or express too many preferences. He learned to be bland and affable, though he grew weary of the way his friends always competed for his notice. He couldn't help the raw energy he exuded. He did not know how to make himself unseen. His only privacy could be found in total isolation, and he loved to be alone.

When each of the kids turned fourteen, their father taught

them how to drive. It was a birthday tradition. He took the lucky child to an empty parking lot to practice, and then led them through the surrounding neighborhoods. He was patient and unflappable in the face of near-misses, lurching brakes. His calm voice inspired his children's confidence, as it did the confidence of his constituents.

Artie was a natural driver. He wasn't nervous. Since he was ten, he'd been driving go-karts on a track and golf carts in the gated communities where his friends lived. He learned quickly and soon became comfortable with the pedals and the gearshift and the mirrors, the sense of the car in space. It was a Lexus, four years old, and normally they would have traded it for a new model, but Bertrand had kept the car for this purpose, for his boy to learn.

Artie had assumed he would be a decent driver, but he was surprised by how much he liked it. Loved it. A sense of power and freedom surged in him, a taste of independence, even with his father riding shotgun. He felt something new, as well: a sense of protection, of privacy. The car was like a force field around him, an impenetrable energy shield like in the comics he loved. In the car he did not have to perform. He could simply go. He could *be*. Adults were always telling kids, *Just be yourself.* Until Artie learned to drive, he never understood what that meant.

After the first few lessons he began to sneak out at night. He would wait until his parents retired to their bedroom suite, inserted their earplugs, turned on their white noise machine, closed their blackout curtains. They made it so easy it was almost like a kind of permission.

At first when he took the car out he limited his excursions to thirty minutes, and stayed on the sleeping neighborhood streets of Lower Garden. But as he gained confidence, he permitted himself farther distances. He drove to his school, which was on a busy street and required traveling through several well-lit intersections and stoplights, navigating past other cars.

He parked on Palmyra, killed the engine, and got out. He had not expected to find the school so changed. It was an entirely different place at night. Its brick facade and high windows radiated a cool and ancient aura, like a ruin. His steps echoed. During the day it was loud and abundant with color, voices, bells ringing on the hour, bright bulletin boards and clutter. Walking the grounds at night, he noticed the building itself, the architecture. He trailed his arm along the brick, listening to his footsteps and the sounds of traffic and cicadas. The smells were familiar, reassuring. He did not think once of the possibility of being caught. He'd never been so calm and free of worry, so connected with his surroundings.

Does every place have this in it? he wondered. This alter ego, this secret life. Does every person? He tried to imagine his friends as they might exist when he wasn't around, what they might do or think when they weren't trying to impress him. I'd probably like them better, he thought, undergoing an odd kind of beautiful melancholy, a generous, expansive sadness for himself and everyone he knew.

He thought about his family, particularly his mother. Did she also contain this alternate universe of silence? He could not conceive of it. She was the same no matter who was around. It was easy for her to be photographed, to be interviewed, to give speeches in front of a luncheon. She was always cheerful, pretty, and energetic, until she fell into bed at nine thirty. She was like their dog Bear when he was a puppy. He would run in circles and chew up everything he could reach until the moment he fell asleep, often midchew, a destroyed sock in his mouth. His naps were pure. He could not be woken. Artie used to try. He'd tickle Bear, pick him up, wiggle his little legs around, but the dog would not alter his steady breathing or open an eye. Bear was a regular grown-up dog now. He'd turned out normal. He went on runs in the early morning with Artie's mother and lay around the rest of the day.

Artie underwent a pang of loss for that puppyhood, gone forever. He'd been in third grade when they got Bear. His younger siblings probably couldn't even remember the era before Bear's existence. How different all our lives are, he thought. None of us can begin to touch one another, not really. He realized not a single person knew where he was at that moment.

In the inner courtyard of the school he found a pencil. Low on the brick wall, behind a stand of ginger plants, he wrote his initials. No one would notice it, but he could look at it during the day and have a connection to the otherworld. After that he returned the pencil to the edge of the sidewalk where he had found it. He drove home and snuck back in.

CHAPTER 13

Since the day they'd cleaned out the fridge, Oliver had started seeing those Art Guidry ads everywhere. There was a new one with a puppy on it, right there on a postcard in Lane's stack of mail. Lane had mentioned something about blood and a boy a few times over the years. Always before, her words had the quality of a half-remembered scene from a dream. Washing blood off. Finding clean clothes for the kid in the middle of the night. When he asked questions about it—Who was this, now? When did that happen?—Lane grew aloof, abstracted. Long time ago, she would say. It's not important now.

This outburst with the television was the first time he'd heard this talk connected to anything concrete. Maybe she really knew this guy, this politician. Oliver had never paid much attention to politics. Far as he could tell, all those fuckers were dirty and not a one of them represented his interests. He didn't think Lane cared about politics, either. He knew for a fact that she did not vote. She'd mentioned the guy's mother, maybe they'd been friends back in the day.

He sorted through the rest of the mail, a pile of bills and a pile of junk, and left them on the table before doing laundry. It wasn't really a part of his job. He was an assistant, not a god-damn maid. But he worried about Lane on the basement steps. He wondered if it would be worth it to relocate the washer and dryer upstairs. They would fit in the pantry, but it would be a major disruption. He couldn't see talking her into a renovation now. Maybe once the on-site painting started, when she'd be out of the house most of the day. He should ask around, meet with a contractor and get an estimate.

He came up from the basement to find Lane leafing through the mail. She pointed to the campaign ad.

"This guy again," she said.

"Yeah, I saw that. What's the story with you and him?"

"Why do you care?" she said.

"My love for gossip is boundless."

Lane laughed. "It was a long time ago," she said. "He was a kid."

"Was he friends with your daughter or something?"

She gave him a warning look. He saw that bringing up Louise was a mistake as soon as he said it. Lane never talked about her.

"Sorry, just curious," he said.

"Go be curious somewhere else," she said.

"This is the guy you said was covered in blood, right? Was he in some kind of fight?"

"Did I say that?"

"Yeah, you did. I think it disturbed the fuck out of Ava."

"Oh, well. That girl."

"Yeah, tell me about it. He got hurt or something?"

"It wasn't him. The blood was somebody else's."

"Whose?" Oliver said.

"I never asked. He's one of those people who get away with things."

"Like what?"

"Who knows, these days. He's running for office, isn't he?" She crumpled up the postcard and tossed it across the table. "I'm sick of seeing this shit. Twenty years of nothing. Now he's everywhere."

"So this thing with the blood was twenty years ago?"

"Are you smoking that, or what?" she said.

Oliver glanced at the pipe in his hand. "Sorry," he said, handing it back.

She took it with her to her studio.

At least she hadn't gotten upset this time—she'd been so pale when she saw the commercial, and it worried Oliver. He wanted to find out the whole story. He'd told Ava not to pay attention to what Lane had said, but really, it disturbed him quite a bit. This guy had done something fucked up. Oliver wanted to know what it was.

After his errands, he went home and looked up Art Guidry online. He scrolled through the campaign website—the guy was thirty-four years old, which would make him fourteen twenty years ago, when the thing with the blood happened. Oliver skimmed the prose, a bunch of bullshit about continuing his family's tradition of service. There was a photograph of his father, longstanding city councilman Bertrand Guidry. Maybe this was Lane's connection to the family. Either that or Art was friends with Lane's daughter.

Art had graduated from some boarding school in Connecticut, but before that he had gone to Jesuit High School in New Orleans. Oliver knew lots of boys who'd been kicked out of Jesuit, for low grades or bad behavior, and ended up at other

Catholic schools, including De La Salle with Oliver. But he'd never heard of anyone being sent away, not unless their whole family moved. Not finishing high school in New Orleans would be a liability if you were running for office, Oliver thought. The first thing everybody asked was where you'd gone to school.

Oliver called the administrative office at Jesuit. When the secretary answered, he gave his name. "I'm a journalist," Oliver said. "I'm writing profiles for the city council candidates, and I'm looking for information about a former student. Arthur Guidry."

"Oh, I've seen his ads," the woman said.

"Yeah, they're all over the place. I'm trying to find out what he was like back then. What clubs was he in, sports, that kind of thing. And when exactly he was there. I think it was around the late nineties."

"You could start with the yearbooks," she said. "We have a complete set in the library. Come by the office before five. My name's Maxine, I'll be at the front desk."

"Thanks, Maxine. That's great. I'll swing by this afternoon."

Oliver hung up, took a shower, and put on a button-down shirt and slacks, a convincing outfit for a journalist, he figured. He drove across town and parked in the visitor lot at the school. He contemplated the building for a moment, feeling a prickling resentment toward the bratty, entitled Jesuit boys. The school was renowned for its rigorous academics. It was the alma mater of civic leaders, generations of successful men, wealthy, connected elites. Nobody appreciated that more than the Jesuit students themselves. Their arrogance was legendary. Oliver and his friends had gotten into plenty of fights with them when they were teens.

He sloughed off the old schoolboy anger and walked into the building. I'm a reporter, Oliver reminded himself. At the front desk he introduced himself to Maxine, a middle-aged blond lady in a tacky patterned blouse. She appeared to accept his story without question, and Oliver relaxed. He'd always excelled at pretending to be someone else—growing up gay in Catholic school made it second nature. She escorted him through empty halls to the library and unlocked the door.

"The yearbooks are here," she said. "Stop by my desk when you're finished and I'll lock up."

"Thanks a ton," Oliver said. "You're a great help."

He took a guess with the 1995–1996 yearbook, and found the guy right away. Arthur Guidry had started eighth grade in 1995. He appeared in the rugby team photo, the French Club, and the Comic Book Club, where he was listed as president and founder. Along with his school photo and the clubs, he appeared in several candid shots, laughing with older students. What kind of kid was president of a club in the eighth grade? His name was listed on the honor roll, too. An A student, an athlete, one of those nerdy popular types who was good at everything. He must have been full of himself, a real go-getter. One of those assholes.

Oliver found the next year's volume, and it was more of the same. But in 1997–1998, he was missing entirely. So was the Comic Book Club, Oliver noted. Art Guidry must have left before they took class portraits his sophomore year. Something must have happened in 1997. He shelved the books and walked down the hall, eerily quiet in the summer.

He took the two volumes to the front office, held them up and smiled at the secretary.

"Thanks for your help, Maxine," he said.

"Oh sure, hon. You find what you needed?"

"Partly. Can I make a few copies of these pages?"

"Sure." She punched in a code for the copy machine behind her desk. "All yours."

Oliver copied Artie's pages. "It looks like he was here for two years, eighth and ninth grade, then he left. Do you know why?"

"I sure don't," she said. "That was before my time. Maybe it wasn't the right fit? Jesuit is a demanding—"

"I know," Oliver said. "But he was an honor roll student. He was in a bunch of clubs. He seemed to fit in fine. Could it have been a discipline problem?"

"I suppose so."

"Could you check? Do y'all keep files on former students?"

"Gosh, I'll have to see what kind of information I can give you. There could be privacy issues. My boss is on vacation this week. I doubt I'd be able to get you an answer until he gets back."

"That's too bad," Oliver said. "I was hoping to get this story out sooner. How about folks who were around back then? Are there any teachers who might remember him?"

"Mr. Boyle, maybe? He's about to retire. He teaches freshman algebra."

"That's great. What's the best way to get in touch with him?"

Maxine typed something, scrolled with her mouse, and pulled a notepad to her. She copied down a phone number and email address and handed the page to Oliver.

"I can't thank you enough," he said.

"Good luck with your story," she said. "Send me the link when it's published." She handed him a business card.

"I will," Oliver said. "Take care."

In the car he dialed the number Maxine had written down and left a voicemail for the old teacher. Online he found the number for the boarding school in Connecticut and called it, but a recording said the offices were closed. It was after business hours on the East Coast.

He examined the photocopies. The reproduction of the

photos was terrible, but the print came out clear, and it was the names he really cared about, anyway.

At home he smoked a bowl and flipped through the photo-copied pages, studying the group photos with their lists of names. He started with the Comic Book Club. Only five boys were in it that first year, and seven the next—the same group plus two newcomers. Oliver checked the other pages to see if there was any overlap. Two boys from the club were also on the rugby team both years. Friends, then, most likely. He googled the names and found one of them, it was probably him, still in town and working as a prosecutor. Oliver looked up the website of the law firm—it had been around for ninety years and had offices in the CBD, right on St. Charles. Fucking lawyer, Oliver thought. Great. Fucking Jesuit boys. He wrote down the address and phone number. He'd call in the morning.

Oliver sighed. He missed Lane, suddenly, the old Lane, the Lane who threw those parties and caught his eye across a room of giddy drunks shoving shrimps into their mouths. She'd give him this smirk, widen her eyes, make him laugh. She couldn't care less about money, status. She used to make fun of her clients and their preening, their god-awful taste. But she could charm them, too. The Uptown yoga moms, the Newman PTA bitches, the snotty gallerists, and all the rest.

Oliver finished getting ready and drove to John's. They were supposed to meet John's friends for dinner at Pêche. Oliver was not looking forward to it. John's friends were so pedigreed. Food writers and professors and presidents of nonprofits. They sat on boards, compared notes about their kitchen remodels and ex-pensive vacations.

John insisted on including Oliver in this circle. You belong there, he said. They love you. But Oliver didn't buy it. Why would they love him, a high school dropout? Maybe they fantasized they could still access some youthful, unpolished, half-dangerous world. Or who knows what they thought. Mostly he suspected they wanted to fuck him, or they pitied him, or both. Usually he drank too much and said outrageous things, put on a show. It was a way of compensating, but he wasn't in the mood for it tonight.

CHAPTER 14

1997

The day after Artie's night visit to Jesuit, the school hummed, vivid and alive, in a way it never had before. He could see past the bright bulletin boards with their wavy corrugated borders, past the maps and posters, and the other boys, his classmates and friends, each jockeying for social position, or hoping not to be noticed, each preoccupied with their little lives.

Artie had seen the other school, the school at night. He thought of it, suddenly, as the real school, the school's true self. He had seen its bones. He looked past the decorations, listened underneath the too-enthusiastic tones of Mrs. Hinds, the art history teacher, explaining the kiln process of firing clay. He knew the school's empty heart, its articulated skeleton, the soft whisper of its soul, independent of the teachers and children who used it in the day.

Artie took careful notes about the history of pottery in the Western tradition, though he was barely listening. He thought of his initials on the wall behind the ginger plants, but he delayed going there. He made a rule for himself, a single glance when he happened to pass by. Art Appreciation was on another side of the building, and English and history in the afternoons kept him away from that entrance. To go out of his way and seek it out felt coarse, antithetical to the spirit of his secret.

He went through the entire school day without seeing it. At home he finished his schoolwork and played with his little sister while his mother went to fetch his brother from soccer practice. He set the table before being asked and read in his room after dinner. He felt himself operating like a smooth machine, powered by the simple act of writing on the school's night wall. He fell asleep at nine and woke before his alarm the next morning. Friday. French class after lunch. The walk from his locker to class would take him past the spot.

He tried not to think about it, to simply let it happen—a casual glance on his way in the building. But the day jerked and stuttered as though some grit seized the gears. Irritability set in. Even before he passed the mark on the brick, he could tell it would be a disappointment. The exhilaration of the day before felt childish now, embarrassing. The school was merely the school, it had no secret heart, no affinity for Artie. Nothing special existed just for him.

Though he'd gotten plenty of sleep, he felt drained, couldn't concentrate. The morning was math and biology, and it droned on, irrelevant, enervating him further. At lunch his friends were scheming a sleepover plan for the weekend, at David's. David's parents had a pool house with a big-screen TV, a Nintendo, a popcorn machine, and they usually left the boys alone out there, staying inside, drinking wine with their friends.

Artie had no enthusiasm for the sleepover. The graffiti loomed, he'd see it soon. More than anything he was ashamed of his former excitement. He saw now how stupid it had been to put off looking at the marks on the wall. He should have gotten it over with yesterday. He said something to his friends—sure, yeah, he'd ask his mom if he could spend the night.

The bell for afternoon classes finally rang, and Artie rose, went to his locker, and gathered his textbooks for the afternoon. He exited the doors under the covered walkway. He had no desire to see it now, the evidence of how lame he'd been. Out with a car at night, he could have gone anywhere, but the place he came was school. It was a move a dumb kid would make, predictable, pathetic. The secret drives still held promise for him. The problem, he understood now, was his destination.

Though Artie didn't care about the graffiti anymore, some impulse compelled him to complete the cycle he'd begun. He sidestepped to the edge of the sidewalk that gave him the best view. He kept his posture straight, his eyes ahead, until the moment he was abreast of the wall, right before the entrance of the Language Arts Building. He flicked his gaze to the left, without slowing down or turning his head, and gained the briefest impression of smudged letters on bumpy red brick. And then he was inside the building, then sitting in class, straightening his books on his desk, and then the bell rang, the teacher started talking. Artie felt blank, emptied out. At least the thing was done.

That night he went to David's and stayed up late, eating junk food and playing video games. He did his best to hide his boredom and frustration. Restlessness stirred in him, and he ignored it until he could be alone.

Sunday his dad offered to take him driving. They practiced in the usual parking lot and his dad commented that Artie seemed much more confident than before. The compliment touched him—his dad's attention was so often divided.

"I wish I could go on the streets," Artie said.

"It'll happen soon enough, bud. When it's time, you'll be ready."

"I'm ready now."

"It's a whole different deal on the road with other cars, son."

"I know."

"Your mother will be sending you out on all kinds of errands. I bet you'll be sick of it within a week."

"Doubt it."

His dad checked his watch. "Better get going," he said. "Pull into a parking place and let's switch."

"Can we get a map?" Artie said. "So I can learn my way around."

"Sure, bud."

At a gas station they picked out a folded paper map of the city. Artie studied it later, marked the places he knew: home, school, his friends' houses, the church, the park where they played soccer. The movie theater where his parents dropped him off with his friends the first time he'd been in public without an adult, when he was eleven. It had taken him months of pleading before his mom consented. Artie was sick of everything in his tiny existence. Sick of being young.

He regarded his room, the blue-checked curtains that framed his windows. The table under the window that had been there since he was little. It was wood painted a cheerful yellow, chipped on the corner. He'd chipped it on purpose, years ago, to see what would happen. His mother hadn't even noticed. The map was the most grown-up thing he had ever owned. Even his beloved collection of Spider-Man comics was suddenly a thing he would one day leave behind, without regrets.

CHAPTER 15

Lane and Ava entered a period, about halfway through the summer, in which they got used to each other and settled in to a more or less comfortable routine. Lane rose late, usually after eleven, and went straight to work. She preferred to shift from sleep directly into isolated creativity, with as few distractions as possible. Ava learned how she liked her coffee, and set it down in front of her without a word.

Later, in the afternoons, Lane emerged from her studio. Sometimes she appeared to be carrying on a conversation she'd been having in her head, figuring out a problem of composition or a clever way to incorporate the windows. Sometimes she spoke of memories, people she used to know. Ava tried to piece together the context, but usually she had no idea what Lane was talking about. She smoked marijuana all day long. Ava worried that it made Lane forgetful. She had heard this in school, in a special seminar they held for eighth graders in the auditorium. A police officer came and showed them a PowerPoint with illustrations of different drugs and their dangers. But Ava wasn't sure which parts were true and which parts might be exaggerated to scare them.

Ava was reading in her room one day when she heard Lane's voice.

"Louise," Lane called.

Ava waited, listening. After a minute, Lane came in.

"Louise, come when I call you," she said.

"I'm not Louise," Ava said.

Lane's face reddened. "Don't talk back," she said. "If your father were around—"

"What?" Ava said. "You never even met him. Did you?"

Lane appeared to lose her train of thought, and when she spoke next it was with a shrill anxiety in her voice.

"What are you doing here?" she said.

By now Ava was used to her grandmother's moments of confusion.

"I'm Ava," Ava said. "Louise's daughter. I'm staying here."

"Someone's been in the house," Lane said. "My candlesticks are missing."

Ava had figured out already that this kind of talk was unfounded—according to Oliver, there had never been any break-ins in the house or even in the neighborhood. *That's just old people paranoia,* he had said. Still, it was best to humor her.

"What candlesticks?" Ava said.

"They were Great Aunt Jennette's," Lane said. "The silver ones from the mantel."

"I'm sure they're here," Ava said. "What do they look like?"

Lane reached across the dining table for her sketchbook and opened it to a clean page. She began to draw, quickly. Ava watched the image appear, startling in its realism: a bulky candlestick, encrusted with sculptural clusters of grapes and leafy vines. Lane added fanciful details and shading, and a few graceful lines indicating the mantel and the old wooden clock that sat at its center. Ava recognized the clock, but she'd never seen the candleholder before.

Seeing Lane draw was a profound pleasure. Ava loved her grandmother at these moments. She watched as Lane sketched, unnecessarily, the second candlestick, identical to the first. The two matching objects were rendered so exquisitely they enacted a kind of gravitational pull on the page.

"They came from Aunt Jennette's, on Carondelet. Mama had them since she was sixteen. Where the hell are they?"

Ava was startled by the vehemence of this question. Lane had seemed utterly absorbed by the drawing, and Ava thought she might leave off with her worrying, but she did not. Ava could never tell when Lane's mind had touched upon something in the present or the remote past, or something imagined, and she gave up trying to guess.

"They're valuable," Lane said. "Quite old."

"Well, let's look for them," Ava said.

They began in the hall closet, pulling out ancient boxes loaded with odds and ends.

"Hey, check this out," Ava said, upon finding a music box tucked behind books on a shelf.

Lane opened it and they watched a Bakelite ballerina perform a slow spin as a metallic waltz played.

"This was Uncle Arthur's. It must have belonged to his sister who died."

"Who's Uncle Arthur?" Ava asked.

"He was Papa's great-uncle," Lane said. "He lived here for a bit after his wife died. Grandmama took care of him in his old age. Those paintings in the hall were his, too."

"Which ones?"

They went to the hall to examine the paintings, a group of

four framed watercolors of street scenes, horses and buggies, ladies with parasols.

"He did these?" Ava said. They were much different in style from Lane's, more impressionistic.

"No, no. He bought them. We never had another artist in the family."

"You're the only one?"

"Far as I know. Your mother was never interested in anything creative," Lane said.

"She could draw," Ava said. "But not like you. She cooked, and baked. She made amazing cakes."

"She was a good mom, wasn't she?" Lane said.

Ava nodded, familiar tears clogging her throat. Lane put her arm around Ava's shoulders and drew her into a half-hug. They stood silently before the paintings. Lane rarely touched her or expressed any affection. Ava held as still as possible, not wanting it to end.

"That doesn't run in the family, either, being a good mother," Lane said. "You were lucky."

Ava hadn't thought about it that way before. She wasn't sure she felt lucky.

"What shall we have for dinner?" Lane said.

Together they leafed through the drawer of takeout menus. Ava called in their order while Lane smoked a bowl, the candlesticks forgotten. After dinner Ava took the music box to her room and listened to the waltz. This house, Ava thought. The past was all around them, disheveled layers of generations. No wonder she gets mixed up.

CHAPTER 16

Oliver hadn't had any luck getting through to the old teacher, Mr. Boyle, or Stuart Davis, Art Guidry's lawyer friend. He'd tried calling, left them voicemails. Tried making an appointment with the lawyer, but his receptionist named a date four weeks out. He'd showed up at the offices, to see if he could barge his way in, but the lobby security wouldn't even let him on the elevator. He circled around the building on foot and found the exit to the parking garage. He figured partners in the law firm would be close to the lobby entrance. He was right, and not only that, but the reserved spaces were marked with people's names. It couldn't be easier. He found Davis's car, a flashy white Jaguar, and left a note on it.

Oliver checked his watch. It was almost four. Maybe the guy kept regular office hours. Oliver decided to check back around five o'clock, see if he might be leaving then. Oliver strolled down the block to a hotel bar. It was happy hour, why not? He had time for three drinks, as it turned out. Feeling pleasantly wobbly, he strolled to the parking garage a little after five. His note was still tucked under the windshield wiper of the Jag. He leaned on a clammy concrete pillar nearby. He'd give it fifteen minutes, tops, and then go home. To entertain himself he tried to guess what the lawyer would look like now. A paunch, a wedding ring digging into his fat finger, thick wavy hair. Dark gray suit, blue tie. Blue or yellow.

When a slender man with thinning hair approached the Jag Oliver almost dismissed him, so thoroughly had he convinced himself of this image. The man beeped the car unlocked and opened the door.

"Mr. Davis!" Oliver called, walking over. "Stuart Davis?"

"Yes?" The man turned and faced Oliver.

Oliver introduced himself. "I'm a reporter," he said. "I'm doing a piece on Arthur Guidry's high school days. You were at Jesuit with him, right?"

"Yeah."

"I would love to ask you a couple of questions. It won't take but five minutes, I promise."

"Listen, I've got to be somewhere. If you call my secretary, she can set something up."

"I tried that already," Oliver said. "I know you're a busy man. But look, I'm under deadline. Really, just a few minutes. I swear I don't normally stalk people in parking garages."

Oliver laughed, charming, self-deprecating, flirting a bit. The lawyer hadn't gotten in his car yet. Oliver could tell he almost had him.

"Are you still friends with Artie?" Oliver said.

"Sure."

"He's running an impressive campaign. I'm trying to write a piece that shows his ties to the city, his history here. Some of my colleagues in the press, the way they portray him . . . it's like they don't understand how much he cares about New Orleans."

The lawyer was nodding, listening.

"I think he could do a lot for the city," Oliver said.

"Aren't you folks supposed to be impartial?" Stuart asked, raising an eyebrow. Was he flirting back?

Oliver smiled. "Freelance," he said in a stage whisper. "Let me buy you one drink."

Stuart glanced at his expensive watch. "Okay," he said. "I can do one."

They walked around the corner together to a different place, Stuart's suggestion, a fancy wood and leather sports bar with lots of high-end bourbons. The bartender served them with a single giant cube of ice that gave off a wisp of vapor in the glass. John would probably like this place, Oliver thought, then realized he could never come here with John because he might run into Stuart and have to explain.

They settled into a booth and Oliver got out the notebook he'd bought for this purpose.

"That's great that you're still friends," Oliver said. "You and Artie. Even though he left Jesuit."

"Well, we did lose touch for a while, when he left. It was sudden. But you know how it is. High school. Those bonds never leave you, do they? Where'd you go to school?"

"De La Salle," Oliver said. "I didn't have the grades for Jesuit, I partied too much back then. So what was Artie like in school?"

"Same way he is now," Stuart said. "Impressive. High energy. Popular. Everybody liked him, and he was nice to everybody. I'll tell you what he was like—we were on rugby together. Most of the guys played rugby because they couldn't make football. But Artie chose the rugby team because he loved it. He read about it, researched it. He somehow got these videos of British documentaries about the history of the game. These were VHS tapes, he must've special ordered them. God, we watched those things over and over. Artie made the whole team feel proud of what we were doing out there on the field. Even the stoners, and the great big boys who just liked to fight. He had us all convinced we were involved in something magnificent. Everything he did was like that."

Oliver took notes, for verisimilitude. "This is great info," he said. "Exactly the kind of thing I was hoping for. So what happened sophomore year? You said it was sudden?"

"Yeah," Stuart said. "One day he wasn't at school. We figured he was sick or something, but he never came back. We never saw him after that. Then like a month or two later I got a letter from him. An actual letter in the mail, remember those? From his boarding school out east."

"Did you ever find out why he left?" Oliver said.

"No. You should ask him, I guess. I figured it was some kind of breakdown. Artie never got in trouble, his grades were great. I don't know. He never talked about it."

"When exactly was this?" Oliver asked.

"I remember he missed homecoming. We'd been calling him for days and no one answered, the whole family must have gone with him. It was strange not to hear from him. The rugby team was planning this body paint thing for the game—you know, paint ourselves blue and wear some kind of skimpy drawers, I can't remember exactly." Stuart smiled at the memory. "We didn't end up doing it. It was Artie's idea, and he was supposed to get the paint, we were planning to get ready at his house and then go to the game together. When he wasn't in touch about that, we started to think something really bad might have happened."

"What does he say about it now?" Oliver said. He'd written down *Homecoming, soph year.*

"Nothing. A lot has happened in our lives since then, obviously. And he's very busy with his campaign." Stuart finished his drink.

"You sure it was that week that he left school?"

"Definitely," Stuart said. "We didn't have time to come up with any other plan, on such short notice. God, I remember the shame of it, like our team had let down the whole school. Rugby always did something big for homecoming. At Jesuit, they drill that into you. Respect for tradition, moral uprightness. The teachers constantly asking us 'What do you stand for?' It was intense."

"Yeah, I've heard about that," Oliver said. Jesuit had always sounded like a cult to him.

"The coaches, everyone was disappointed in us. I remember it well."

"Lot of pressure," Oliver said.

"Yeah. Maybe it was too much for him." He checked his watch. "Shit, I've got to run."

"I won't keep you. I really appreciate this," Oliver said.

"Happy to, really. Let me give you some other folks to reach out to. May I?" he gestured to Oliver's notebook.

"That would be fantastic," Oliver said.

Stuart wrote down a couple of names and phone numbers, then stood and shook Oliver's hand. "A pleasure to talk with you," he said. He had a faraway intense air about him. Oliver wondered if it was from the bourbon or thinking about Guidry.

"Thanks for taking the time," Oliver said.

At the door Stuart turned back to Oliver and said, "He'll win, you know."

Oliver nodded. He thought so, too, but he didn't really care.

At his apartment he researched the dates of Jesuit homecoming. For the past few years it had been the last full week of September. Probably it was the same back then, too. This town and its traditions.

The next morning he called the school in Connecticut and found the office there eager to help. He was transferred to the director of student affairs and went through his spiel about the article he was writing. "He started as a sophomore in fall of 1997. I understand he came in the middle of the term. I wondered if you could tell me the exact date?"

The guy said, "Yes, that's right. He came to us in the first week of October. He moved into the dorm on October fifth and began classes the next day."

"That's a bit unusual, isn't it?" Oliver asked.

"Yes, it is uncommon. But it happens. The parents' schedules can conflict with ours—some of our pupils are sons of senators, ambassadors, professional athletes. We try to accommodate unusual circumstances."

"Guidry was enrolled in school in New Orleans and left suddenly. Do you know why he switched?"

"I couldn't say," the director said. "But it seems he adjusted well. His grades were excellent. He was involved in lacrosse, rugby, the student council. Junior year he was elected student council president. Usually that distinction goes to seniors who have been here all four years. Mr. Guidry looks to have been an exceptional student."

"Yeah," Oliver said. "Doesn't surprise me. Thanks for your help." He ended the call. He was sick of hearing about Artie, but at least he had narrowed down the dates. Whatever happened, it went down sometime in late September. A fight? A nervous breakdown, a suicide attempt?

Oliver poured himself a cup of coffee and sat at the computer. The *Times-Picayune* archives were online now, he'd used them before to do research for Lane. He searched news items during that last week of September, typing in keywords like *assault, altercation, accident*. He skimmed through the results. Most of them referred to trials under way for previous crimes, or descriptions of drunken bar fights between adults, with many witnesses.

He found a reference to a Chalmette man killed in a hit-and-run. Wayne Sampey's corpse was found on the street at four thirty in the morning. The guy was forty-one and had been born in St. Bernard Parish, lived there his entire life. He had an ex-wife, two kids, a job at a pawnshop. Poor bastard. Oliver noted it and kept looking, but there was nothing else in the archive that could explain a fourteen-year-old boy covered in blood. Oliver did a search for Sampey's name, to see if the cops ever found who did it. As far as he could tell, they never prosecuted anybody.

An unsolved hit-and-run in the middle of the night, the same week Artie left school. It was a possibility. But then again, what was the boy doing way out in Chalmette in the middle of the night? Did he even know how to drive? If Artie was driving the car, what happened to it? Whose was it?

A thing like that would be enough to hustle the brat out of town, and someone like Artie's dad would be able to do it, for sure. He probably had cops in his pockets, could call in favors. And if there were no witnesses, then it would simply be a question of getting rid of the car. It could be smashed in a junkyard by dawn that same day. A city councilman could have that done. Oliver knew those kinds of guys, guys like Guidry and his dad, how they operated.

Oliver would need to double-check, to find out if Sampey's death really was related to Guidry. He still didn't quite see how Lane figured in. He'd need to find out more from her, and that would take some finesse. He'd have to wait for the right moment.

Meanwhile a plan was already forming in Oliver's head. His instincts told him he was on the right track. Oliver had always had a knack for this stuff, recognizing what shards of information could be important. Like spotting a valuable antique in a jumble of crap at Goodwill. He had an eye. He could have been a detective, or a politician, if things had turned out differently. But he would never have gone that route, even if he'd had the option—he was no hypocrite, pretending to help people. Oliver helped the people he cared about: Lane. John. His auntie, before she died. Himself, he supposed. It was a short list.

CHAPTER 17

Ava rode along the river under heavy cloud cover, past corner liquor stores and brightly painted houses with narrow yards. She was somewhere in the Irish Channel, or maybe Lower Garden. She didn't understand what marked the differences between one neighborhood and the next, though everyone else seemed to see these borders as obvious and important.

She approached a small park with a basketball court, a playground, and a couple of skate ramps. She rode along the edge of it, then walked her bike over to a shaded bench. As soon as Ava stopped riding her body became drenched in sweat. The court was empty, but a dad and two little kids were over by the playground. Some skaters were sprawled on the steps near the skate ramps, idly rolling their boards back and forth. They looked the same here as they did in Iowa—teens with asymmetrical haircuts, wiry bodies, the same kind of baggy clothes and flat-soled sneakers.

One boy stood, started doing a few casual kickflips. Ava pulled a water bottle from her satchel and drank. She took out her book and half read, half watched the skaters. One of the little kids on the playground started to cry and the dad gathered them up to leave. They all held hands as they crossed the street and entered a lime-green bungalow. The boy who was doing kickflips skated over to the ramp and jumped it. His board rolled out from under him, headed in Ava's direction. She stood up, stopped it with her foot, and sent it back to him.

"Thanks," he called. "You skate?"

"Kind of," Ava said. "But I haven't practiced in a long time."

"What can you do? Can you ollie?"

"I used to."

"Come on," he said. "Let's see."

She walked closer to him, leaving her stuff at the bench. He sent the board over to her and she caught it with her foot, mounted it, stood unsteadily. She tried to get a feel for the board, balancing for a moment. She kicked off and sailed a few feet, turned, stumbled, laughed, got back on.

The boy laughed, too, but not in a mean way. She stood on one end of the board, lifted it a couple of times, and attempted a clumsy ollie. She got hardly any air, but she didn't fall.

"When's the last time you were on a board?" he said.

"Two years ago, I think. But I was never that great, anyways."

"No, you're good. Especially for being out of practice."

"Thanks," she said.

She pushed the board to him. He flipped it with his foot and caught it in his hand, one easy, graceful movement. Ava wished she could be so at ease, doing anything. The streetlights over the park flickered on and shone down on his straight hair.

"I'm Jase," he said. "And that's Ben and Lizzie and Tru." He pointed to his friends.

Ava introduced herself and waved to the others, who were coming over to them. They each nodded at her, said hey.

"Getting dark," Ben said. "We doing this or what?"

"We're about to split," Jase told Ava. "You want to come with us?"

"Where?" Ava said.

"You'll see, come on."

The girl, Lizzie, looked at Jase. "Is she cool?" she said.

"Yeah, Liz, she's cool," he said, laughing.

Ava walked her bike alongside them. Lizzie and Tru zoomed ahead on their boards, jumping curbs and broken bottles in the streets, weaving into an alley lined with Dumpsters and an occasional folding chair propped by a back door. Ben followed close behind them and Jase hung back with Ava. He asked her about the bands she liked, where she rode her bike, what YouTubers she subscribed to.

"I don't watch videos that much," Ava said.

"That's cool, most of them are lame. You like to read, right?"

"Yeah."

"What was that book you were looking at?" he said.

"I found it in my grandmother's house," Ava said. "It's these crazy stories. I picked it up cause I thought the cover was cool."

"Can I see?"

Ava pulled the book from her bag and handed it to him. They looked at the cover, a stylized turquoise and purple tessellation. In the failing light, their heads bent close together.

"Oh, it's like peacock feathers, right?" he said. "Is it about birds or something?"

"Not really," Ava said. "In one of the stories this Bible salesman comes to a farm and everyone thinks he's really nice and kind of dumb, but he ends up stealing this woman's wooden leg."

"That's wild," Jase said. "What for?"

"I don't know. He likes it, I guess. He tells her he got someone else's glass eye one time."

"What a weird dude."

"Yeah."

Ben coasted back to them. "Lizzie found a dream spot, come on."

"Dream spot for what?" Ava said.

"She's a writer," Jase said. "You'll see."

He dropped his board and pushed off, following behind Ben. Ava rode after them down the alley. At the corner Jase waited for her, held up a corner of chain-link fence that one of the others had bent away from its post.

"Hurry," Jase whispered. "Leave the bike, come on."

Ava leaned her bike against the fence and ducked under, aware of Jase's proximity. His body smelled of clean sweat, like hay.

"Follow me," he said, still in a whisper.

She stayed behind him. The others were up ahead, single file, running between the building and the fence until they stopped, suddenly, and Lizzie unzipped her bag. In the dim light ahead of Jase and the others Ava could make out some cylindrical objects in their hands, and then Ava understood: spray paint.

"She's so dope," Jase whispered. "Wait til you see."

The wall was clean white stucco, the side of a bungalow-turned-corner store. Ava saw a round Pepsi sign protruding from the front of the building. It lit up from the inside and read ED'S LIQUORS EGG BREAKFAST. Because she was alongside the wall she could not see what Lizzie was making, but Ava watched her arm move, heard the hiss of the can above the cicada buzz of night.

Ava had seen murals everywhere in the city but had never thought about them being made like this—spontaneous, sudden. Lane spent so much time sketching and thinking be-fore she painted anything. Ava didn't know that art could be this immediate. Watching Lizzie's direct expression of creative energy, Ava felt a new sense of possibility. Heat radiated from the sidewalk and the air and Jase's body in indistinguishable, overlapping waves. Ava breathed it all in, inched forward until she was almost touching Jase's shoulder.

He reached for her arm, tugged her closer, so she could see. The paint was dark purple against the white wall, a cartoon outline of a long-eared rabbit with wheels instead of feet. It was almost as tall as Lizzie, and looked like a robot version of a rabbit, with a squared-off belly. Next to it Lizzie drew a symbol, an eye with a square iris.

"That's her tag," Jase whispered in Ava's ear. "Robot eye."

"It's awesome," Ava said. She loved watching this thing happen, this transformation from a regular wall to a piece of art. Seeing these shapes flow out of the can. Everyone should do this, Ava thought. There should be paintings on all the buildings. The world would be so much more interesting.

Farther down the wall Tru was throwing up tags, messy scrawls of black paint, the same indecipherable letters over and over. Ben held Lizzie's backpack in one hand, looking out into the street beyond.

He gave a low sustained whistle, distinct from the other night sounds. Lizzie dropped her paint can and turned to Ben, who jerked his head toward the direction they'd come. Jase ducked, ran back to the hole in the fence, pulling Ava behind him. They had to run single file, Ava between Jase and Ben, Lizzie and Tru at the rear. Jase got to the hole in the fence and grabbed his board, pulled the chain-link up, shoved Ava through then followed. She scrambled out of the way of the others.

From the sidewalk a man yelled, "Hey! You fucking kids!"

They were all in the alley now, the other four already on their boards, yelling, Go, go, go.

The man came roaring toward them, his unbuttoned shirt billowing at his sides. Ava turned to Jase and the others, but they were around the corner, out of sight, the sound of their wheels receding.

"Stop," the man yelled out.

Ava froze.

"I'm calling the cops," he said. "So sick of this shit." He held his phone in his hand.

She looked at the wall through the fence, saw the marred stucco, understood all at once the transgression. This was somebody's place, it belonged to somebody. Ava was horrified at what they'd done, how stupid she'd been not to realize it was wrong.

"Sir, I am so sorry," she said. "I didn't know—we can clean it. Oh god."

"We? Who the fuck's we?" he said. "Your hood friends scattered."

"I'll fix it," Ava said. "I really am sorry, I didn't know what they were gonna do."

He squinted at her. "Why didn't you run?" he said.

Ava shrugged.

"I just met them," she said. "Please don't call the police."

"Well, somebody's got to take care of my wall."

"I can paint over it," she said. "I painted my bedroom last year. I mean, I helped. I remember how to do it."

The man looked her over. She was young, he saw, younger than he'd thought at first. Something about her made him aware of himself. He began buttoning his shirt. He'd been in the middle of getting a late dinner together, tomato salad, cold cuts from the fridge in his apartment at the back of the store.

"Alright, I'll call your parents," he said. "Bet they don't know you're out roaming with those punks."

"My parents are dead," she said. Straightforward, simple, just a statement of fact. But then she started to cry.

Maybe she was a little con artist after all, he thought. He ignored the tears. "Well, I'm calling somebody."

"I stay with my grandmother," she said, through her tears. "You can call Oliver, he helps her out."

She gave him the number. He dialed, explained the situation.

"Alright," the man said, "He's coming. Christ, I'm sick of this bullshit. This neighborhood used to be different."

"Can I—" she said. "Is it okay if I get my bike?" She pointed down the alley, where a cruiser leaned on the fence.

"You have a bike. And why are you still here?" He shook his head. Something was off with this one, he couldn't quite tell what. "I'll get it, alright. Hold on to it til this guy shows up."

She nodded, stayed where she was as he walked down to the bike. She could run even now, but he didn't think she would. There was a small backpack in the basket, no lock, no nothing.

"This bag belong to you, too?" he called.

"Yes."

He walked the bike back to her. "You can't just leave this lying around, girl. You should lock it. Keep your stuff with you."

"Yes, sir," she said. "I usually do."

The rain that had threatened all day finally started falling, large warm drops that made a racket.

"Shit," he said. "Come on."

He took the bike around front and unlocked the shop, pushed the bike inside, and parked it in the aisle of canned goods. The girl hesitated behind him, standing in the rain, already nearly soaked.

"Come in," he said. "Look, I got nieces. Younger than you, but. Come out of the weather."

Ava stepped over the threshold into the dark store. The man turned on the overhead lights, fluorescent tubes that illuminated a room filled with shelves of liquor, groceries, a wall of refrigerated cases in the back. Near the door, a counter with three stools, a cash register at one end, a small griddle behind it.

"Have a seat," he said. "My name's Ed. You hungry? You want a soft drink, a Coke or something?"

"No, thank you," she said.

"Sure you do." He pushed a roll of paper towels toward her. "Dry off a little. If you want."

She took a couple of towels from the roll and blotted her face and arms. He walked over to the cases and got her a cold can of Coke, put it in front of her. He went behind the counter and stayed there, so as not to rattle her further. He twisted the cap off a bottle of sweet tea and said "Cheers."

She opened the Coke and took a sip. He'd never seen a more miserable child in his life. She had stopped crying, at least.

"Why you running around with those kids anyway? You're not one of them."

"They were nice to me," she said. "I feel so stupid."

"Hey, you know, we all make mistakes," he said.

He felt sorry for her. She didn't have the hard look, the tough sheen of most kids her age, with their earbuds and their quick sarcasm. How would a girl like this make it in the world?

The door chimed. They both looked to see this man, must be Oliver. The girl looked more miserable than ever.

"Well, well," Oliver said, closing his umbrella, dripping water on the mat. "Always knew you'd end up in juvie, it was just a matter of time."

"Hi," the girl said.

He held out his hand to Ed. "I'm Oliver," he said. "So what's the story here?"

"Ed. Look, I don't think she meant any harm by it. The others, those kids are no good, the ones who got away. She stayed and offered to help. But the thing is, my wall."

"She offered to help," Oliver said, smiling.

Ed thought for a minute, studying the man and the girl together.

"Now who are you again, to her?" he said.

"Personal assistant to her grandmother." Oliver explained who Lane was, described his job while Ed watched the girl. She looked so sad. Something didn't feel right, just letting her go with this guy.

"I know this place," Oliver said, looking around. "I got an ex used to live around the way, Jeff Gruen?"

"I haven't heard that name in a while," Ed said. "We went to Franklin together."

"He loved your breakfast sandwich. He graduated what? '03?"

"Yeah, a year behind me. He was always a decent guy," Ed said. "Hell of a hitter. Where'd you go to school?"

"La Salle," Oliver said. "I would've finished in '06, but."

Ed nodded. Katrina year.

"Look, I'm sorry about all this trouble," Oliver said, gesturing to Ava. "A hundred bucks take care of it?"

Ed nodded, accepted the money.

"Ava, go on and put your bike in the trunk. Here's the keys."

They watched her wheel the bike out the door, into the rain.

"I appreciate you being so understanding about this," Oliver said. "If I had to deal with police or whatnot, this would've been a shittier night."

"No problem," Ed said. "Look, man. Is something kind of like, wrong with her?"

Oliver laughed. "She's alright, she's just from Iowa."

"Huh." Ed nodded, taking this in. "Well, tell her to be more careful who she gets mixed up with."

"Oh, I will."

Oliver went outside and got in the car. Ava sat looking straight ahead, already buckled in. He put the car in gear and headed back to Lane's.

"So let me get this straight," he said. "You pick up some gang of, what, street thugs?"

"They seemed nice," Ava said. "They were just kids."

"Okay, so your nice friends vandalize this dude's store, this regular, hardworking corner store dude—he could've shot you or something. You're lucky he felt so sorry for you."

Ava stared at the rivulets of rain pouring down the window.

"So then your nice, sweet new friends run off, and then—" He had to stop talking, he was laughing so hard. "Sorry," he said. "Ah, god, this shit's funny. Okay." He caught his breath. "So instead of running away with your new friends, you stay behind and tell this guy you'll *repaint* his *wall*?"

"I swear I didn't know the place belonged to somebody. I mean, I thought it was like Lane's murals, there's murals and graffiti everywhere around here. I thought it was okay."

"You realize that if you took off on your bike, you could still be with your new best buds, and I could still be relaxing at home, and it would've saved your grandmother a hundred bucks."

"I'm sorry," Ava said.

"Don't be sorry," Oliver said. "You little weirdo. I haven't laughed this hard in a long time."

"Thanks for coming and getting me," she said.

"I'm not going to let this go, you know. I am going to keep making fun of you for this indefinitely, you realize that?"

"Okay. Fine," she said.

"Thug," he said.

"Shut up."

"Delinquent."

"Shut up."

"Should we stop by the store and pick you up some spray paint?"

"Shut up."

But she was definitely smiling now, he could hear it in her voice. He felt proud of her, in a way. Maybe she'd turn out to be a normal kid after all.

CHAPTER 18

1997

Artie studied his city map. His dad had offered to hang it on the wall of his room, but Artie said no. He'd already become partial to the portability of it, the accordion fold, the way it resisted if you bent it the wrong way. He liked how it could fit in his backpack, or the drawer in his bedside table. He flipped it back and forth, reading the street index, linking up familiar buildings and landmarks with the tiny grid.

It was maddening to be so close to these places—houses, buildings, restaurants, city blocks—and not know them at all. He memorized routes, loops that began and ended at his house and took him through neighborhoods he'd never been to.

Over the weeks and months his secret excursions led him out to Chalmette, New Orleans East, Riverbend, Back-of-Town. He explored Tremé, the Marigny, the Bywater, even took the bridge across one night and drove around Algiers. The streets were tranquil. Sometimes he thought he was the only one awake in all of New Orleans.

He enforced a strict schedule: Don't leave before 3:00 A.M., be home before 4:45. His mom woke up at six to run with the dog, and he wanted to be asleep in bed before then. He kept a notebook alongside his map and filled it with a shorthand of his own invention, detailing dates and routes and what he had seen. He also marked the places on his map, tracing streets in pencil. He envisioned one day the whole map covered over in graphite lines. He did not go out more than once a week, usually on a Tuesday or Wednesday. He didn't talk about the trips to anyone.

Artie's parents and his teachers expected him to do something important—go into politics like his dad, or medicine, or become a CEO of a big company. He wished he could be an explorer. He knew everything was already mapped out, he wasn't naive. But that didn't prevent him from wanting to discover things for himself.

Some nights the drives left him lonely. Moving through dark streets was no way to really see a place. Each one of these houses contained a family of people he would probably never meet. And even if he did, how could he ever hope to understand what their lives were like? People showed you what they wanted you to see. He thought about how well he knew the fat palm tree in his own backyard—its jagged outlines, its texture, its dusty smell. Everybody had a thing like that, a tree or a view, something they lived alongside, that no one else would ever truly know. He thought, too, about his own bedroom, how its character changed when somebody else came in. No matter how close you were to others, people's individual realities stayed impermeable.

Once he pulled the car over on a residential street of small tidy houses in New Orleans East. He got out of the car and walked, thinking he'd maybe circle the block. He was especially sleepy that night, and the darkness of the lake along his left had unnerved him. He needed to feel his feet on the ground, that was all. But before he'd gone thirty feet a dog began to bark from somebody's yard and he ran back to the car and drove home.

When he lay down in bed, finally, at four thirty in the morning, after having parked the car in the exact spot in the driveway where his older sister had left it that afternoon, carefully closing the door to make the least possible sound, and sneaking back up the stairs, he found he couldn't sleep. He lay there trembling, not from fear of the dog or being caught, but out of frustration. Where was life and why couldn't he touch it? How could he get at it? Even though he was already fourteen and a half, almost as tall as his dad, practically a man, as his parents frequently commented, he shook and wept like a little kid, finally falling asleep after dawn, just before his mother came to wake him.

Artie got used to not sleeping enough. He thought he was keeping up with everything, school and rugby and chores, but his mom noticed his fatigue. He heard her talking on the phone about him. He could tell from her tone and the way she laughed that her friend Mina was on the other end of the line. They jogged together in the mornings, went to movies together, gossiped about everyone. *He's slouching around,* Artie's mom said. *Maybe he's going to grow again. I just bought him new uniforms a month ago.*

She didn't seem alarmed, but any extra attention made Artie nervous. After that conversation, he went to bed a half hour earlier each night, willed himself to rest. If his mother found out about the excursions, it would be a disaster.

He lay in the dark, thinking about the bumpy potholed streets curving along the river and shooting out to the lake, lined with houses and people, with strange lives and juxtapositions and stray animals and centuries of history all piled up, crazy colors muted by the darkness and yellow streetlights. The city was out there, and Artie wasn't in it. He resolved to be careful, more careful than ever.

CHAPTER 19

Oliver's plan was taking shape, but he still needed to run some things by Lane. He got a chance a couple of days later. The girl was in her room, out of the way. She'd been subdued since Graffitigate, the little criminal.

He found Lane in the kitchen. She seemed lucid enough.

"I checked into that thing with Art Guidry," Oliver said.

"What thing?"

"The car wreck, the accident."

"That's ancient history."

"I know, I know. It's shitty that he got away with it, though. Makes me want to not vote."

Lane laughed, like actually laughed. "Like you were going to? They don't want you to vote, anyway. Nobody wants you to."

"He killed that guy, didn't he? Out in Chalmette."

"I wasn't there," she said. "I didn't see anything."

"But you know what happened, don't you?"

Lane sighed. With Bert gone, there was no one left to protect. It had happened so long ago.

"I knew about Chalmette," she said, "but not the rest. Bert went out there to deal with the car, left the boy with me."

"Bert his dad?"

"Yeah."

"You were mixed up with him?"

"What's with the questions?"

"Fuck, Lane. Must have been a nightmare, is all. And he got away with it."

"Sure he did. Course he did."

"Think if something like that happened to me. Or Little Prairie Girl. They'd put us in jail and throw away the key, don't you think?"

Lane shrugged. "He had rich parents, powerful parents. And they loved him. That's how it was."

"But what about the poor dead guy?"

"What, you think I should have called the cops?"

"No. I would have done what you did."

"Then what are we talking about?" she said, and walked away, back to her studio.

On his errands that afternoon Oliver detoured past Artie's headquarters, parked and strolled past the storefront festooned with campaign posters. Staff people and volunteers were sitting at desks with piles of posters. The pretty blond wife the guy had found back east, the one on the postcard, she was in there with her little girls, a toddler and an older one, maybe five or so.

The wife was chatting to a lady at one of the desks, and then the man himself came out of an inner office. Oliver watched Art Guidry kneel down and hold out his arms, and the two little girls ran to him, jumped on him, and he scooped them up. These types. Oliver considered their blond heads and their little pink embroidered overalls, and the wife in her flats and skinny jeans and on-trend utility jacket. If he experienced any hesitation about the plan, it dissolved once he got a look at the family. They had everything.

He figured a simple note would do. Back at Lane's, he paid some bills, returned a few calls and emails to her potential clients, balanced the checkbook. He waited for Ava to leave on her bike and made sure Lane was busy. Not that he was worried about Lane, she didn't notice anything he did.

He typed out the instructions—leave $10,000 in a backpack in the alley behind this closed-down sandwich shop in the Warehouse district. He'd be able to watch from the window of the bar across the street. He typed a date and time, and the threat. If the money wasn't there when he asked, he'd go to the media, he'd tweet about it. He implied that he knew the whole story, that he had evidence. Oliver had never done anything like this before, blackmailed somebody. The ease with which it was happening seemed to undercut its shadiness. He thought of it as an experiment. Maybe it would work.

He deleted the document once he had a hard copy. He remembered at the last minute not to touch the paper—could paper hold fingerprints? It could have Lane's or Ava's fingerprints on it already, but Oliver figured that was unlikely, since nobody touched every single piece of paper in a stack when they put it in the printer. The edges, maybe. But the thought gave him pause. He figured it was a low-risk situation—worst case, the guy wouldn't come through with the money, and that would be that. Oliver was sure he wouldn't go to the cops. But to be on the safe side, he put on the yellow rubber cleaning gloves from under the kitchen sink and opened a new pack of paper.

He printed out an envelope, too, which took forever to figure out how to do. He printed the address on the wrong side twice before getting it right. He addressed it to the campaign headquarters and marked it PERSONAL. Last thing he needed was some campaign volunteer opening this shit. He got it sealed and stamped, though not neatly—the ill-fitting gloves made it tricky to handle the paper. He put it in his back pocket, gathered the misprinted envelopes, and burned them outside on the balcony. He touched the note in his pocket, felt the weird energy coming off of it. His heart started skipping beats, pounding hard. He steadied himself with a shot of bourbon.

In the car, he headed toward the mailbox on Henry Clay, but then changed his mind. He shouldn't mail it from Lane's neighborhood. He thought about where to go, and then the idea hit him. Chalmette. Near where it happened. It was out of the way, but there'd be no traffic at this hour. WWOZ was playing decent music and he kept it on that, rolled his window down.

He drove along Tchoupitoulas, feeling the heavy body of the river on his right, before turning lakeward. He took I-10 East and came down Paris Road, searching for a mailbox to drop the letter in. He finally saw one, pulled over, stuck it in the slot. He pictured little Artie out driving in the middle of the night, and wondered what it must have been like for him. He was what, fourteen? No license, sneaking out, doing god knows what out here. Hunting for drugs, meeting a girl, planning some dumb prank. And then a guy comes out of nowhere, jumps in front, or the kid lost control of the car, or something. In order for him to be covered in blood, he must have parked and got out and touched the guy. Maybe even held him, watched him die. Something like that would fuck with a person.

Oliver took Judge Perez Drive back to his neighborhood. It was done now. All he'd have to do is wait. Guidry wouldn't get the letter for another two days. He thought about where he could go, what he could do with the money. Too jumpy to stay home, he walked up to the bar and drank whiskey. An older couple who'd been there for hours started talking to him. They were the kind of sunburned white people who were way too into reggae, but they bought him a couple of rounds. When the woman started asking him to dance, Oliver split. Part of him felt like he was still driving—the letter wrinkling in his pocket, passing under one Chalmette light pole after another, thinking about car crashes.

CHAPTER 20

Artie sat at his desk in the inner office of the headquarters, performing a meditative task in which he retraced the moments of mundane routine before he had opened the envelope. He breathed, thought through waking to his alarm, shutting it off, rising from the bed. Marisol had stirred, murmured something to him before nestling into her pillows. He took himself through his morning jog with the new dog, trying to recall as many details as possible—where the puppy stopped to do his business, which cars had been parked on his block. He recalled the sweat, which instantly covered his skin in the early morning humidity. In the outer office his staff answered phones, typed emails, sent volunteers out on door-knocking trips. They stapled signs to wooden stakes, they piled up boxes of church fans printed with his image.

Artie continued his process of long slow exhales, recalling his shower after the run, the sounds in the house, his children talking to his wife in their chirping little voices, the steam condensing on the marble tile. He remembered the texture of the towel on his skin, the sound of the dry cleaner's plastic as he peeled it from a fresh shirt.

He wasn't doing this meditation to calm himself. Artie was already calm, he could control his emotions better than anybody. It was one of his talents, this unflappability. He'd developed it as a teen, cultivated it as an adult.

But the envelope had a strange property. Once he had read its contents, he noticed an odd collapsing of time. The twenty years between today and the event that had prompted him to leave New Orleans, to leave his family, to go out on his own—those decades shrank down to nothing. Artie marveled at this effect, the thoroughness of it. Here he was, not twenty minutes from the place where it had happened, and though he had operated under the belief that he was not that child anymore, that he had become someone different and better, someone powerful, he realized now this belief was an illusion.

He needed his context back: the skin of his wife's soft cheek, which he nuzzled on his way out; the girls' sticky hands, the weight of little Pearl hugging his leg and sitting on his foot as he poured a go-cup of coffee, chanting in that impossibly high pitch, *bye daddy bye daddy bye daddy bye daddy;* the color of the traffic cones he maneuvered around, they were still tearing up the avenues, there was no way to avoid the construction, it was one of his talking points, how to update the infrastructure more efficiently, with less disruption to neighborhoods; the smells of the sidewalk outside the bakery on Magazine where he picked up pastries for the staff; the weight of the pink box, heavy with filled brioches, butter already seeping through the cardboard as he carried it to his car; sunshine bouncing off the plastic beads in the trees above his parking place.

Artie noticed, with nearly perfect detachment, that as he approached the recent memory of walking in the door and handing the pink box to Kirk in exchange for the pile of mail containing the envelope, he experienced new physical sensations.

Clamminess, a swimmy quality to his vision. *Stay in the moment,* he told himself. He closed his eyes. He stood in his headquarters, an important man, still young, bursting with energy, ready to do great things for the city he loved, holding a stack of mail addressed to him, surveying the office bustling with people who devoted their time and energy to him, who believed in him.

Artie watched Marley, his volunteer team leader, organize her people. They were delivering yard signs today, in every neighborhood from Riverbend to the Lower Ninth. His name and his face repeating in yards from the river to the lake. After today, anywhere he went in the city, he would see his own image.

The letter threatened to reveal details of the accident to the *Times-Picayune,* Nola.com, Twitter. He considered his options. He could ignore the letter, let whatever happened run its course. Maybe the letter writer would follow through on the threats, and maybe not. He wondered what the newspapers might do? The story would be tempting in its scandal, but there was no evidence. Reporters required facts, required proof. They might, feasibly, discard the whole thing. Artie had contacts at the paper and at Nola.com, he could possibly finesse that situation. Twitter was another matter. If the story got any traction, the media might report on it. But would it make a difference with the voters? Maybe not. He could still win. His campaign could get out ahead of it, he could break the story himself. He'd been a child, after all, he made a mistake, he let his father handle it the way he thought best.

But this would mean he'd have to tell his wife, Marisol, who knew nothing of the incident. She was a lovely, warm person, a great mother, energetic and kind. Everything in their lives together thus far had gone exactly how they planned. He had no idea how she would react to this news, to the ordeal this might become. And he'd have to tell his mother, who believed the story his father had told her twenty years ago, that Artie had taken the car and wrecked it, had been arrested, that Bert's friends at the police had kept it off the books, that the best thing for Artie was to take him out of his social environment, get him a new start at a new school. His mother hadn't been the same since Bert's death. She was frail, too thin. She deserved better than this story coming out. No one would believe she hadn't known. He couldn't do this to her, not now.

The easiest thing was to do what the letter said. Artie didn't like the idea of being beholden to the whims of a stranger, a criminal. But getting the money together would be simple. He could pull ten grand from his money market account, tell Marisol he was investing it. It was an investment, in a way. He could think of it as a campaign expense. He would swing by the bank before lunch.

CHAPTER 21

1997

Lane sat up waiting, in her summer nightgown, feet bare, a glass of bourbon in her hand. She hadn't seen Bert in weeks, long enough to really miss him. The anticipation played through her restive body. Louise was sleeping at a friend's house. She'd finally left, after an unpleasant evening of grouching about homework and some permission slip she needed signed for school. Lane had picked up a new project, an elaborate ceiling in a new boutique hotel. There was so much prep to do for the job that she was tempted to go back to it now, but she might not hear his arrival from the studio.

She stepped out to the balcony. The backyard lay below, beds of white caladiums glowing dimly in the streetlight. She'd sweated tirelessly in the spring burying the bulbs. They looked pretty now, but when she saw them she thought ahead to the fall, when she'd have to dig them back up. Why did anyone bother? Maybe she'd replace them with perennials next year. Or pave the damn thing over. Lane's grandfather would never have entertained such a thought. He'd loved the garden. Thomas had, too. He'd helped her with it in the brief years of their marriage.

There were moments Lane wished she had someone else. Not a husband. Just another adult who could share some of the work.

Louise was such a handful, always needing rides, new school uniforms, home-cooked meals, poster board for the science fair. Left to herself, Lane could subsist on peanut butter sandwiches and wine, but she cooked a balanced diet for Louise—fish and vegetables, red beans, gumbo, casseroles. Lane needed to pick up some shrimp and onions for tomorrow. She could do that after the PTA meeting.

Here, finally, were the headlights of his car. Lane was half-drunk on whiskey, her head teeming with irritating details, lists of things to buy and do. She watched him open the gate, silently, and follow the path to the balcony steps. He was a shadow in the night yard. She sipped her drink and watched him. God, he was good-looking. He came up the steps, crossed the balcony to where she stood.

He took the glass from her hand, swallowed the rest, set it down. He moved closer, his hand at her hip. At his touch she realized how lonely she'd been. He lifted the gown off her and she stood naked, his eyes like warm air on her skin. She was sober now, alert, entirely present. She waited, letting him look, prolonging the moment. A test to see how long it could last.

He spoke, his voice cracking on the syllable, Christ. In wonderment, in desire. She couldn't hold still any longer, reached for him, tugged his belt free of its buckle, her hands scrambling for his fly. He still wore his suit pants, shirt tucked in, though he'd left his tie and jacket in the car. She groaned aloud when she touched him with her hand. He shifted forward, pushing her against the outside wall, lifting her onto him.

He was silent, slow, watching her face. His Lane, always so collected. People who didn't know her thought she was cold. He liked to make her face change, liked to see her lose control.

Nothing excited him more. He thought of her when he was in the office, when he was with his family. He loved her composure, loved that he knew exactly how to break through it, to shatter that surface. He could open her, undo her, make her beg, as she was doing now, incoherent whispers, urgent. He slowed, held her still and watched her face as he eased out, teasing her. She grabbed for him, digging her nails in. Please, she said. She looked like she might cry. Her voice grew higher, louder.

Hush, he said.

She obeyed, her eyes filled. She whimpered softly. He pinched her nipple. She made no sound but her body spasmed. Tears now rolling down her cheeks. He gave her what she wanted, slowly, the length of him sliding in and out. He loved to spank her, turn her skin red, but now, when they had to be silent, he did other things. Pulled a fistful of her hair, yanking her head back. Pinched her. He could do anything to her in these moments, her need for him would accommodate anything at all. He bit her breasts, sucked at them.

She was writhing, panting, goose bumps covered her skin, her nipples puckered into hard stones. He wanted to fuck her ass but she wouldn't be able to stay quiet. He held himself tight to her, let her writhe on him.

"Don't make a sound," he said into her ear. He waited until she nodded, agreeing, and pulled her closer, pushing his cock all the way in. He put a finger in her ass, knowing what it would do to her. He kept himself still inside her and moved his finger in and out, holding her tight. He loved to feel her come like this— tense, straining. He kissed her, gave her something to do with her mouth, her tongue. He tasted the whiskey on her breath and sensed her, finally, succumb to the waves of orgasm. It wracked her body, her muscles clenched around him and he let himself fuck her steadily. She was barely there, close to passing out. Her eyes half-closed, her mouth slack. He pinched her, this time on the soft underside of her arm. She flinched, awake now.

Look at me, he whispered. Again, she obeyed, her face serious. He kept the steady rhythm, felt her squeezing him as he pulled out. God, she was perfect, amazing. He let her do what she wanted now, ride him, rub herself on him. He held her up, her legs wrapped around his hips, bouncing on his cock. She quickened her pace; she was going to come again. The second one was always smaller, less intense. She was more aware of herself. He didn't care about watching her this time. He lifted her off of him, waited while she found her legs, she was trembling but able to stand. He turned her around and bent her over the railing, shoved himself inside her. He reached around, flicked at her clit. It didn't take much before she started to shudder. She pushed her ass up toward him and she looked so dirty and beautiful he stopped trying to hold back.

After, he made her kneel and clean him with her mouth. She hated to taste herself on him, but she did it willingly, docile now. She found her nightgown and put it on. Bertrand pulled his pants up, fixed his fly, left his shirt untucked. They went in the kitchen and shared a drink. Sometimes they talked after, or lay down together, but he saw how sleepy she was. He put her in bed and kissed her, then took a shower and left the way he'd come, silently through the back garden.

CHAPTER 22

Oliver couldn't believe how smoothly the thing had gone. He hadn't held this much cash in his hands in years. He'd forgotten the rush of carrying around that kind of money. Its dizzying potential.

He'd gotten to the bar across from the alley an hour early and snagged the front booth facing the window, a perfect view. By the time the sleek Audi turned in and parked, he had a nice buzz going. He watched Guidry leave the car with a bag, return without it a moment later, and steer up the street. Oliver finished his drink, paid his tab, and ambled across to the mouth of the alley. There, on the ground behind an unused Dumpster, was the canvas bag. He scooped it up and circled the block to his car.

He counted the money once, then again. Ten thousand, in hundreds, exactly like he'd instructed. He wanted to spend it immediately. He took the freeway out to Metairie and parked in front of Causeway Coin. The place looked like a dump from the outside, but they had a reputation for being fair. Inside Oliver went straight to the counter of luxury watches.

They had plenty of vintage Rolexes and Patek Philippes, but Oliver was immediately drawn to a Vacheron Constantin

Patrimony with a platinum case, taupe face, and black alligator band. It was superb. Oliver could never have afforded it new, but pre-owned, it was a possibility. They had it listed at $11,500, but Oliver talked them down. They were persuaded by the bag of cash. He handed it over and watched the owner fuss over the watch, polishing its perfectly polished face, fitting it into a gift box, polishing it again. Oliver ached to have his hands on it, he had to restrain himself from reaching across the counter and grabbing it from the guy. Finally the man handed him the box and he was out of there, driving, the watch tucked in his lap.

When he got to John's store it was nearly five, but John was stuck with a customer. Oliver waited, the box in his hand. The customer was one of those smooth-haired older ladies weighed down with chunks of jewelry. She was giving John a lecture on silver marks, as though John didn't know all about them. He was patient, even with these arrogant clients, people with fragile egos and money to spend. He'd imitate the worst ones over dinner with impressions so accurate he could make Oliver weep with laughter.

Finally they finished up. The lady left without buying anything.

"How do you not strangle them?" Oliver said.

John smiled. "She'll be back. She's going to buy the Swedish armoire."

"The painted one?" The armoire would bring twenty grand at least, and selling it would free up valuable space in the shop. It had been there four years already.

"She has taste, at least," John said.

"Hey, I got you something," Oliver said, as though he'd forgotten and just remembered.

"Please say it's candy, I'm starving."

"Sorry. It's not candy. Here."

Oliver handed John the box and held his breath while John opened it. He was half-afraid the box would be empty, the watch still back in Metairie, the stacks of cash a figment of his imagination. But there it was, the gleaming Vacheron Constantin, sleek and elegant.

"Oh my god," John said. "Oliver, are you serious?"

"Like it?" Oliver said.

"It's the Patrimony," he said. "Manual wind?"

Oliver nodded.

John took it out of the box and turned it over. "It's gorgeous. The weight of it. My god. Transparent caseback. Look."

"Let me help you put it on."

Oliver stepped in close, took the watch from John, and buckled it around his wrist. The leather offset the platinum buckle exquisitely. John held his arm out, turning it this way and that, admiring.

"Jesus," Oliver said. "That is one sexy watch. It's perfect on you."

He couldn't take his eyes off John, Oliver's gift strapped to his wrist. Nervous energy roved through him. He touched John, bewitched by the image of his own hand on John's tanned forearm, the platinum case flashing. He tightened his grip, a new feeling of ownership building. It was after five, past closing time. Oliver went to the door, bolted it, and flipped the CLOSED sign out, then returned to John, who watched with interest, taking surreptitious glances at the watch on his wrist. They'd never fucked in the store before but Oliver wanted to now. He rarely thought of himself as John's equal, but the gift gave him a new sense that anything was possible.

Later, they went to Red's Chinese for dinner and sat at the bar.

"But how could you afford it?" John asked.

"You worry too much. I got a little bonus."

"It's too much," John said.

"Hey, don't flatter yourself, dude. It's pre-owned."

John laughed. "I love it."

"Good. Me, too. Listen, I've been thinking about something. You know I haven't taken a vacation in like two years. We could go out of town. She owes me some days off."

"What about that weekend at False River?" John said.

"Ah, yes. The wondrous False River." It was a joke between them, a god-awful two days at John's friends' lake cabin. On the inside their place resembled a suburban condo, outfitted with cast-off furniture that was still nicer than anything Oliver could afford for his apartment. The lake was peaceful, he guessed, but it smelled like fish guts and there was nothing else around besides a Walmart.

"Let's take a week. Go to the Caymans," John said. "Or Hawaii. Or New York."

"New York," Oliver said. "I'm into that idea."

"I haven't been to New York in, what? Five years? Can you really get away?"

"Now that Ava is here, I feel better leaving Lane. She won't be on her own."

"Good. She's a grown woman, you know. She managed to survive without you for decades."

"I know, I know. And the kid will help out."

Oliver deserved a break from both of them. He was worn out by Ava's sadness, it was starting to affect his mood. She'd lost her mother, sure, but it was a drag to be around someone so morose. Who wasn't fucking sad? Life was shitty for everyone, and Oliver was no babysitter, no therapist. They'd be okay on their own for a week.

CHAPTER 23

Lane got up early, in the grips of a familiar momentum. The project was starting to shift, to turn into something more than she had hoped. She had a lunch with the restaurant people later, so she organized her sketches to present her progress, taking pleasure in the way they added up to more than the sum of their parts. This magical coalescence didn't always happen with a piece. It was like falling in love, in a way. The same high.

She heard a tentative knock on her studio door, and the girl peeked her head in.

"Lane, would you like some eggs?" Ava said. "I'm bored of cereal."

"No," Lane said.

"You should eat something, though. What can I fix you?"

"I'm working."

"I miss Oliver," Ava said.

"Me, too. Least he knows when to be quiet so I can think."

"Sorry."

Ava backed away. Lane heard her making noise in the kitchen for a while until finally she left on her bike. The girl disturbed

Lane. Being around a child was strange—children bent time, changed the shape of it. And she looked too much like Louise.

The current project, the Marigny restaurant, was massive, ambitious. It would be her best work. It would stand after whatever was happening to her had finished happening, after she was gone. As she drew, time retreated, twisted, frolicked. Because of the subject matter, partly, the depiction of an era barely remembered by the city's oldest trees and buildings. The past, the past. Memories, coquettish time, like Louise, little Lulu, cavorting in the water at Perdido Bay, those summer trips to the beach. Brown as a nut, staying under for longer than was probable, breaking the surface twenty yards away. Lulabelle, Louise-iana, Ouisie, Lou. Love erupted, broke, a violence no one had explained to Lane and for which she was unprepared. Lane, helpless and bound, alone with love that too often seemed interchangeable with terror.

Louise in her two-piece pineapple swimsuit, yelling Mama, watch! She dived from the pier and came up at the tip of the sandbar, too close to the channel where boats passed. Love took the form of conjured-up horrors: kidnappings, impalings, drownings, accidents. Love crashed into dread, lapped constantly at the shore. The long limbs and strong body of her daughter were so vulnerable. The sharp bones of a gar sliced her foot as she ran on the sand.

Those years killed painting. All Lane's energy centered on her daughter, and when she managed a few hours in her studio she'd felt like a hobbyist, her powers diffused. And for what? Louise left as soon as she was able. At the end of each day, when aches, hunger, or sheer fatigue brought the work to a halt, one thing was clear: that day was never coming back. Lane would try to rest and not think about how every moment of not painting was gone forever. She worked in a state of constant anxiety, in a rush, propelled by engines of panic and denial.

She hated to leave her studio, but it couldn't be helped. She drove to the CBD for lunch with the restaurant group—it was the financial people, not the chef. The chef she wouldn't have minded. She recognized the haunted hungry energy about him, the ambition, his attention always divided between the world's insistent processes and his vision. Today, she was led to a table for three: Lane, and two people in suits she had met before, a man and a woman. The man, Philip, fussed over the wine list, engaged the waiter, asking his advice.

The tedium of lunch. Small talk, food talk. The menu was some kind of Asian fusion thing. She ordered the special without caring what it was. Noodles maybe? Fine. The wine came, and some minutes of discussion about traffic, the weather, and then the entrées arrived. Glass noodles, shredded herbs, unrecognizable. They gushed about the plating. The woman, Myrna, photographed her food before she ate it. She tucked her phone into her handbag and turned to Lane.

"Thank you for meeting with us," she said.

"Oh, sure," Lane said. "It sounded urgent."

"We've had some problems come up," Myrna said. "Issues with construction that are going to affect our time frame."

"Time frame?" Lane repeated, frowning. The words had trouble making sense. Time, framed. Framing time was useless. Time was a figure moving under the surface of the bay and breaking somewhere else, scattering droplets, catching the light. Might's well try to frame water. Your frame would be driftwood soon enough, and rusty nails.

Philip said, "We've had some delays. It's setting us back, we don't know exactly, yet. At least ninety days. We've had issues come up with the historic preservation board, some structural problems with the building. It was a bit of a blow. You know what they say, no telling what's there until you open up the walls."

Lane had never heard anyone say this. "Three months," she said. She was ready to start, she'd nearly completed the prep. Now it would have to wait until fall? Impossible.

"There's another thing," Philip said. "There may be some shifts in the design. We've got the architects and the contractors on-site, working out solutions. We'll have to do some creative problem-solving to stay within budget."

"Old buildings," Myrna said. "You know how it is."

"Once we have the new plans, we'll get them to you."

"So the work I've done?" Lane said.

"We are hoping the changes won't be too drastic," Philip said.

"We ought to have a better sense of it in the next few weeks," Myrna said.

"We should talk about your schedule," Philip said. "We'd like to keep you, we love your work, obviously. It's been a part of our vision since the beginning. But we definitely understand if you don't have the flexibility."

"Definitely," Myrna said.

Finally Lane understood the point of the meeting. They were letting her go. The research, the plans. The weeks she had spent fruitlessly, the hours she'd never get back.

"Lane," Philip continued, "we were hoping to keep you on retainer in event of this kind of delay. But unfortunately any extra funds will be eaten up by the construction fees, the redesign, and pushing the opening back."

"We hope you'll be available when we're ready," Myrna said.

"We hope the changes won't be too extensive," Philip said.

"We won't have anything left in the budget for a redesign," Myrna said. "So when the walls are up, if you're available—"

"And if you can use what you've done already," Phillip said.

"Or adapt it pretty easily, obviously," Myrna said.

They were talking about money. Lane did not give a shit about the money. The lost time tunneled like a wormhole into the irretrievable past. She wanted to leave. She could not abide the rest of the lunch.

The waiter came by and Philip and Myrna asked question after question about the dessert menu. What kind of bread was used for the bread pudding? Baked in-house? What whiskey was added to the sauce? When finally they ordered coffees and a cobbler and, of course, the bread pudding, Jesus, they cared so much about the details of their every aesthetic experience though they didn't comprehend the first thing about what it meant to actually make something. These people were nothing but *eaters*.

Lane stood, disgusted. She smiled thinly. "I'm afraid I have to run," she said. "I can't stay for dessert."

They rose from their seats, promising to keep her updated, to be in touch, and please, if she found herself unavailable, would she be kind enough to keep them in the loop? Of course, yes, best of luck with the redesign, etc., etc., each of them shaking her hand, and finally she was out, walking the two blocks to the pay lot where she'd parked and then lurching uptown through traffic, to her useless sketches.

She didn't know how much time she had left, but it wasn't enough. Losing the restaurant mural terrified her. Three months. Would she even have three good months? Lane knew something was wrong with her, and it was getting worse. She got disoriented. She forgot things, sometimes important things. At times this troubled her and other times she scarcely believed anything was amiss. She wasn't stupid, but she couldn't remember what she couldn't remember. The problems came and retreated at random, as did her awareness of the problems. Being around people was more trying than it used to be, of this she was sure.

CHAPTER 24

The house was empty upon Lane's return. She opened the kitchen door and stepped onto the balcony to smoke, surveying the narrow backyard below, weedy and neglected. She had gardened once, years ago. Such a fruitless task—you could wear yourself out weeding and the weeds came back, you could water and deadhead and then the whole goddamn place would flood and everything in it would die.

Lane wondered if she might be dying. Going to a doctor was unthinkable: scans, needles, condescending looks, the medicines with their awful side effects. She wouldn't do it. She couldn't spare the time, anyway. She realized she had been thinking of this mural as her last piece. Her final, best work. Now it might not happen.

Lane emptied the ashes from her pipe into the patchy grass below the balcony and stepped into the air-conditioning. Somewhere she kept a list of people, potential clients. Perhaps one of them might have a small project for her that she could complete while she waited for the restaurant to get their shit together. A nursery, a dining room, something manageable and ready to go.

On a building that was already built, for god's sake. She would not make that mistake again.

Where did Oliver keep that list? She flipped through piles of papers in her studio, then tried to search the files on the computer, but Oliver had updated the operating system, and the screen looked unfamiliar. Lane would have to wait for him. He hadn't been by lately. It was unlike him, slacking off. She opened her sketchbook, turned to a clean page, wrote the date, Philip's and Myrna's names, the restaurant where they met for lunch, the words "Project delayed 3 months? Possible redesign."

She drew an arrow pointing left, to the previous pages. She shaded it, gave it volume and texture. She loaded her pipe and smoked. Her stomach growled, she'd barely eaten that silly food at lunch. In the pantry she opened a cabinet, took down a can of noodle soup, poured its gloppy contents in a pot. She turned on the burner, tidy blue flames in a circle, and stirred the soup with a wooden spoon. The girl was gone but she had been here; she had a particular way of arranging the clean dishes in the drying rack. Her tidiness, her hesitancy, infected the walls.

Lane stepped away from the sink and the clean plates the girl had washed, the folded dish towel hanging over the oven door. She went down the hall, back to her studio. Papers everywhere, disorganized. Lane paged through them, invoices and receipts and forms and letters. They seemed both familiar and not. She opened her sketchbook to the first few pages, examining each image, birds and bonnets and filigreed carriages.

"Forget it," she said aloud. "The project is delayed." She spoke to the drawings. "You will never be a painting."

Anger roiled in her stomach like hunger. She half-noticed an unpleasant smell and rose to close the door against it. She turned to a clean page and began to draw, from memory, the face of a child, a girl about twelve with shrewd, kind eyes. Straight hair, chin length, combed. Louise was dead. But her face was indelible. Lane knew every facet of it, at every age until seventeen, when she left.

That Katrina fall, Lane was in Missouri and Louise brought Ava to visit. Lane barely registered her granddaughter, a tiny, shy four-year-old—she'd never cared much for small children. Instead she looked and looked at Louise's face. Lane watched her daughter's expression warm when she spoke to Ava. Louise was softer, prettier than she'd been as a girl. They talked about their lives, about the storm, the city, about the farm where Louise and Ava lived. How absurd, living on a farm. Lane always figured that wouldn't last. She hadn't cared about the news, the catching up, even the granddaughter, who hid behind Louise the whole time, apparently getting over some preschool illness that left her recalcitrant.

"She's normally more outgoing," Louise had said. "Still under the weather, I s'pose."

All Lane cared about was her daughter's face, and while they talked in the lobby of this wretched residence hotel, rainlight coming through the window, Lane did not blink, did not avert her gaze for one moment. She was memorizing. Who knew when she would get another chance?

Little Ava started to whine and Louise prepared to go.

Lane said, "You can come visit. You can always come. Bring him, too, your farmer. Once the city comes back."

"Okay, Mama," Louise said.

And maybe she would have. But it took too long for the city to come back. And Lane was still traveling constantly, and then the farmer died and everything got harder. Louise's face. She longed to stare at Louise's face and nothing else until her mind was gone.

Before she finished the drawing a decision had taken hold within Lane. She wouldn't paint on anyone else's walls. Or with anyone else's money. She would use the time she had left to make what she wanted. What she wanted to leave behind. She turned the page and began again. Louise, younger, a different angle, nine or ten years old, long arms and legs, face turned away, gazing at some distant object, one ear and cheekbone defining her face, indelibly Louise, Lulabelle, all the fanciful names.

Lane experienced the confidence and calm that came from knowing the work was right. The details still had to be determined, of course. Canvas? What size? She hadn't painted on canvas in years. But what else was there, without other people's walls?

Her own. The house. Of course. The legacy left her through four generations. The house.

Somehow the house answered, like it could read her thoughts. Maybe she really was going nuts. The front door banged, the house called to her: *Lane! Lane! Where are you?* Lane opened the studio door to the smell of burning, of plastic fumes and shouting. The girl called again, "Lane!" Ava running down the back hall.

More shouting from the kitchen. Lane went in that direction.

"I'm here," she yelled through the smoke.

Ava had already turned off the range and thrown the broken pot in the sink. She was aiming the spray nozzle at a blackened dish towel and a can of Tony Chachere's, melted and burning. The water hit it, sending out enormous plumes of smoke that smelled like cayenne and turned the air to acid. Ava's mouth and nose were tucked into her shirt and she was yelling, "You're okay? You're okay? Open the windows!" Tears poured from Ava's eyes.

Once the danger had passed, Ava collided with Lane in a

fierce hug that caught her off-balance. The girl was stronger than she looked. Her youth was like a brilliant animal.

"Everything's alright," Lane said. "Everything's fine now." Even though Ava had been the one to put out the fire, she seemed to need to hear this from Lane.

They went together through each room, opening windows and turning on the ceiling fans. Lane found a couple of box fans in the basement and set them facing out the door and the window in the kitchen.

"What were you making?" Ava said when they finally sat down on the couch, sweaty in the heat.

"Something new," Lane said, thinking about Louise, the new painting, the walls. But which room should it go in? Compositions suggested themselves between every window and doorway, dazzling Lane with possibility.

"Weren't you cooking something?" Ava said.

"Was I?"

Why was the girl focused on these insignificant concerns? The child Louise's face shone out, perhaps here next to the fireplace, perhaps by the tall windows that overlooked the old live oak out front. Louise used to climb that tree and throw beads to the neighbor kids on the sidewalk. Playing Mardi Gras, just as Lane had done at that age.

"So you probably didn't eat?" Ava persisted. "Me, either. Let's order something."

"Whatever you feel like, hon."

Ava called for delivery from the Lebanese place and poured them each a drink. Wine with ice for Lane and milk for herself.

"What happened?" Ava asked again.

"The project is over," Lane said. "The restaurant job is canceled."

This was not the answer Ava had been looking for, but she understood the gravity of it.

"No," Ava said. "It was going to be so good."

Lane studied her granddaughter, felt an urge to paint her. The house and whatever she made next would belong to Ava. She allowed a wash of gratitude for Louise to ease through her. *Thank you for sending me this girl.*

They slept with the windows open and the fans running. Lane dreamed of her daughter, she dreamed of painting. Ava slept fitfully in the heat, worried about the fire and what it meant.

CHAPTER 25

The next morning most of the smell had dissipated, though every surface was sticky with humidity. Ava shut the windows and turned the air-conditioning on. She was pouring coffee when Kaitlyn called.

"Hi, honeybun!" she said. "How's things?"

"Okay, I guess," Ava said.

"Yeah? Tell me all about *New Awlyuns*."

"It's cool. I've been riding my bike a lot."

"That sounds cool. Getting in shape."

"More like exploring."

"Right. Listen, I have news. I found a roommate."

"What?" Ava said.

"She's cool. A graduate student. I figure she'll be pretty quiet, probably study a lot."

"Is she going to stay in my room? In mom's?" Ava fought the anxiety in her voice.

"Don't get upset, please? I'm taking your mom's room, and this chick, her name's Ginger, she can have mine. Been moving the furniture around, man what a pain."

"I didn't know you were getting a roommate," Ava said.

"Well, I can't afford this place on my own, I was only paying like a third of the rent before. I don't need a place this big all to myself."

"I never thought about that."

"Yeah. Well, it's that or move out, right?"

"What about our stuff?" Ava said.

"I stuck everything in your old room for now. Ginger's bringing her own furniture. But I guess you'll be staying down there, right? Your grandmother can have everything shipped."

"I guess," Ava said.

"Cool. No rush. But I was going through stuff, cleaning up. I found some things I'm gonna send you."

"What?"

"It's these great photos of you and your mom. From before I met you. Your dad is in some, too. I'm gonna send you a package in the mail."

"Thank you," Ava said. "I would love that."

"Listen, it's not like Ginger's replacing your mom. You get that, right?"

"Kaitlyn, *god*. Of course."

"Okay, just checking. You don't have to be all teenager-y," Kaitlyn said. "Anyway, I was thinking, maybe I could talk to your grandmother. You know, check in with an adult. She around?"

"Not right now," Ava said. "She's super busy."

"Alright, well get her to call me?"

"Yeah," Ava said. "I will."

"I gotta run. Keep an eye out for that package, maybe next week."

"Okay. Thank you."

Ava hung up the phone. She would not give Lane the message. If Kaitlyn found out how messed up she was—found out about the fire, or the marijuana, or the problems with her memory, what would happen to Ava? They wouldn't let her stay. So then what? A foster home? Would it be here in New Orleans, or in Iowa, or somewhere else completely? Maybe she would have to live on the street with the gutter punks who always asked for a dollar.

She thought of their apartment in Iowa City, the small tidy kitchen, with her school pictures and report card displayed on the fridge. Louise had taped it up the day it came in the mail. Ava could see it clearly, next to a chunky magnet of a plaster bunny that Ava had once given Louise as a gift. The bunny was too heavy and the magnet not strong enough for its weight, and it periodically slid down the length of the fridge to rest at knee level. Louise loved it and raised it to the top of the refrigerator door whenever she noticed it had sunk. Ava's report card had been excellent, as usual. Five A's, two B's, perfect conduct and attendance.

Louise wasn't the type of mother to give rewards for good grades. Some of Ava's friends got new clothes or cases for their iPhones if they got A's. Louise could not afford those things, but she let Ava know how proud she was. How smart she was. You can be anything you want, Louise said. She had drawn funny little hearts and stars and rainbows in the margins of the report card.

"Mom, that's babyish," Ava had said. "Am I still a five-year-old in your brain?"

"Yes, exactly. You were a cute five-year-old. Remember those purple corduroy overalls you used to wear every day? You'd get mad if I put them in the wash."

"Mom, I'm taller than you, you realize that, right?"

"Nope. Not possible. Besides, what kind of monster doesn't like rainbows."

"Guess I'm a monster then," Ava had said.

Louise wrote in a curly, little girl script, "Mom is proud" at the top of the report card and taped it up. Ava had laughed at her—she'd never gotten anything but good report cards, and to make such a big deal out of it seemed silly. Now, like everything Louise had touched, Ava longed for it. How could she have left it behind? Was it still on the refrigerator or had Kaitlyn thrown it away? Ava pictured the rest of her stuff, and her mother's things piled into her old bedroom. When she had left back in June she hadn't realized she might not see that place again. She clutched the phone and wept.

CHAPTER 26

Oliver arrived Monday morning with a trunkload of groceries and wine.

"Hey, girl, give me a hand," he said to Ava. "There's lots more in the car."

"How was New York?" Ava said.

Oliver shrugged. "Hurry up, there's ice cream melting."

She brought the bags up the steps and piled them at the front door, then went back for more. Oliver's car was always messy, strewn with assorted bags and hoodies, an old blanket, a camping chair. Take-out containers, empty cigarette packs, pay stubs for parking lots littered the dash and the floor. Ava began to gather the empty cups and other detritus to throw away. She unearthed another layer on the floor of the backseat. A porcelain lamp wrapped loosely in bubble wrap, missing a harp and a shade, a pair of tasseled loafers encrusted with dried mud, and a plastic bag that Ava assumed was more old food cartons until she lifted it and felt its weight.

Inside, loosely wrapped in newspaper, was a pair of candlesticks. Ava recognized them immediately. Silver clusters of grapes, black tarnish in the crevices of the design. They were larger and heavier than Ava had realized from Lane's drawing.

Oliver called from the porch, "Iowa, what are you doing out there?"

"I'm cleaning out your car," Ava said.

"Well, quit it. Help me with the groceries."

Ava deposited the trash in the rolling can at the back of the driveway and brought the candlesticks upstairs. Oliver had retreated down the back hall. Ava found him in the pantry opening a case of chardonnay.

"Get the cold stuff in the fridge, will ya?" he said. "Lane still asleep?"

"Yeah, she was up late working."

Ava unpacked the grocery bags. Milk, frozen dinners, bread, a wedge of cheese oozing from its rind.

"Here, stick this in there," Oliver said, handing her two bottles of wine.

After the groceries were put away, she showed him the candlesticks.

"Lane was going crazy looking for these. We searched everywhere."

"Ah, shit. That's too bad," he said. "She gave them to me. She must have forgotten. She asked me to get them appraised, so I took them to John's shop. He just got them back to me."

"Why did she need them appraised?" Ava asked.

"Fuck if I know," he said. "This was a couple of months ago, before you came. I got here one day and the dining table was covered in this old silver and china she'd pulled from the sideboard, and she was talking nonstop about who it belonged to, great-uncles and aunties and such. She went on and on about those candlesticks for some reason. She thought they might be really valuable."

Ava nodded. It was easy to imagine Lane fixated, inexplicably, by some random thing, enlisting Oliver's help. Ava had seen Lane issue orders, imperious, and later forget all about them. Last week Lane had sent Ava on her bike to the corner store for limes. *How could we be out of limes, for heaven's sake, what's Oliver thinking?* She had been furious. Ava brought the limes back twenty minutes later and found Lane immersed in her work. The limes were still unused, going brown and hard in the crisper.

"What's the matter with her, anyway?" Ava asked.

Oliver took the candlesticks, unwrapped them, and put them away in a low cupboard in the pantry.

"She's always been this way, a little," he said. "Impatient, absentminded. She's so fixated on her art, she doesn't notice lots of things."

"I know," Ava said. "She left the stove on the other day. It started a fire. I got home just in time."

"Fuck," Oliver said. "That's never happened before."

"She didn't even notice," Ava said. "She was drawing. And she was really stoned, I think. But I couldn't tell for sure."

"She didn't notice the smoke alarms?"

"They didn't go off," Ava said. She hadn't thought about them until now.

"That's not safe. We can fix that. There's batteries in the corner cupboard. I'll get a ladder."

Ava found the batteries and Oliver brought a folding ladder up from the basement. Together they replaced the batteries. Ava was surprised Lane could sleep through the noise, the creak and thump of the ladder, and the piercing bleat as they tested the alarms one by one.

They ran out of batteries and went to the hardware store to

buy more. When Oliver got in the car, he said, "Aww, man, what happened to my car?"

"Your trash is gone," Ava said. "It was time to say goodbye."

"What if I wasn't ready?"

Ava smiled. "Think of it this way," she said. "Now you have room for more take-out containers and empty Coke bottles."

"Speaking of takeout, we may as well pick up lunch. Where you wanna go?"

"Guy's." Ava loved their shrimp po-boy.

"Guy's it is. Hey, the car does look nice. Much better. Thanks."

"You're welcome."

Over lunch, Ava said, "We have a toaster and a microwave. Maybe we don't even need the stove."

"Interesting idea," Oliver said.

"I mean, when did you last use it? Or see her use it?"

"Years ago."

"Could we turn it off somehow?"

"Let's do it when we get back," Oliver said. "I think we can live without it."

"Hey, I have to ask you something," Ava said.

"Uh-oh, here we go. Now what?"

She told him about Kaitlyn's new roommate. "She wants to ship our stuff, mine and my mom's. But I wasn't sure . . ."

"What kind of stuff we talking about?"

"Boxes of things, some furniture."

"This is some extra shit I'm not getting paid for."

"Sorry," Ava said.

"So this is it, you're moving here? Like permanently?"

"Where else can I go?"

"Back to Iowa?"

"And do what? I'd have no place to live."

"What does Lane say?"

Ava shrugged. "When I ask her, she says, 'We'll see.'"

"Ava, I don't know about this. I really don't. This is beyond my job description."

"Well, I have to tell Kaitlyn something. She asked to talk to Lane on the phone."

"I can imagine how that would go."

"It's not a good idea, right?"

"Look. I think Lane's getting worse. She's forgetful. She gets confused, that never used to happen. She can't take care of a kid."

"I don't exactly need taking care of," Ava said. "I can help. I already am. I mean, if I hadn't been there with the fire . . . You were out of town."

"True," he said.

"And when school starts I won't be in the way as much."

"School. Shit." Oliver would be the one who ended up enrolling her in school, that would be a mess of bureaucracy, he'd probably have to chauffeur her every day. Would there be a carpool? "This is fucked up," he said.

Ava looked miserable. "Oliver, what am I supposed to do? She's my only family. I'm just a kid."

"Now you're a kid. I thought you were all mature, here to help out."

Ava said nothing.

"God, I'm ready for another vacation," Oliver said. "I'll figure it out. But not today, alright? I got other shit to do."

This sounded a lot like Lane's *We'll see,* but Ava said, "Thanks, Oliver."

They finished eating and got Lane's lunch to go. Back at the house Lane was awake and already working in her studio. Oliver and Ava replaced the last few smoke alarm batteries, then Oliver pulled the stove away from the wall far enough for Ava to reach the gas knob and turn it off. They tried the burners and nothing happened. Oliver angled the stove back in place.

It was not until after Oliver left that Ava's thoughts returned to the candlesticks. She wondered if she should show them to Lane, if Lane would even remember they'd been missing. Had she been thinking of selling them? Ava wondered if she needed money. She hoped not. They had enough to worry about.

CHAPTER 27

Oliver had understood for a while that Lane was getting worse, but he didn't like saying it out loud. He'd been in denial, he supposed. Lane would have to see a doctor, and that would be a nightmare, just getting her there. She would resist, say it was a waste of time, she had more important things to do. Oliver knew she was afraid, and who wouldn't be? If it wasn't Alzheimer's it must be brain damage from the solvents and paint thinners she'd exposed herself to. The news would not be good. If things kept progressing like they had been, she'd eventually need in-home care, and that would mean she would have to quit smoking, probably. He'd seen her once during a dry spell and it wasn't pretty. Maybe he could find her a sympathetic nurse, some old hippie who believed in medical dope.

He worried about Lane, he really did. He was the only person who really had the constitution to put up with her, and now that she was slipping, she was even more unpredictable. Ava would be a responsible caretaker. She was steady, despite everything she'd been through. Sharp, too. But what a situation for a kid to walk into.

He was starting to adjust to the idea that the girl would

actually live here. Something was loosening inside him, the tight circle of his affection expanding to include Ava. It was a big change, but then, the job as he'd known it was already over—Lane wasn't the same. Maybe he was ready for something new, anyway.

He'd felt the same way about slinging drugs, back when he first hooked up with Lane. It was a thing he fell into, in Houston, in the turmoil after Katrina. Within six months nearly everyone he dealt with was dead or in jail or gone. He'd come back home with a Jansport backpack of pills stowed in the hollowed-out backseat, and a spare tire packed with hydro. He sailed past the checkpoint state troopers set up in Lake Charles. It was practically risk free, it was common knowledge they never pulled over white guys. His plan was to unload the shit he had and start over with something new, something legal. He was twenty years old and he planned to stay alive and free in New Orleans.

It turned out easy, getting rid of the pills. He sold the whole lot and half the weed to a friend of a friend who knew a bunch of students at Tulane. Fucking college kids loved that shit. It made no sense to Oliver, spending all that money on an education and then spending more to obliterate your wits so you couldn't learn. He didn't get it. But college was never in the cards for Oliver. He was at the beginning of his senior year of high school when the storm happened, and that was that. He took care of his sick auntie in Houston until she died, and after that he needed money, needed to live. It's not like he'd been Mr. A+ student anyway.

Back in the city he had plenty of cash to find a decent shithole of an apartment. He met Lane through a friend of his cousin's and sold her his last quarter bag. When she offered him the assistant job, he said yes.

It had been rocky as hell at first. He'd almost quit on several occasions, but in the end he stayed. She paid well, and mostly it wasn't that hard, not like his buddies doing construction, renovating houses, busting their asses in restaurant kitchens. He finally figured out that she expected him to anticipate her needs, so that she did not have to make any decisions, did not have to think about anything besides her art. As they got more comfortable around each other he came to admire her. She was like family to him: she ignored him, bitched at him, blamed him for things that were not his fault. The difference between his real family and Lane was, she really wanted him there, and she paid him. Plus she could be fun as hell to talk to.

He'd never been around an artist before. Musicians, sure, everybody was a fucking musician. But music was about tradition, community, about getting hammered at the bar. Music ended and everybody was hungover, sore from dancing, and then it all started up again the next night.

But the painting, that was different. The images stayed, you could study them whenever. He saw how long it took for Lane to get a piece right, until it looked as real as a photograph, but somehow stranger. It compelled you to keep looking to be sure it was really only color on a flat surface and not a real lamppost or a vase of flowers or whatever.

She always chose subjects that were imperfect. She painted a bouquet of gardenias, crammed into an old tomato can with a torn label, and the can was real as could be, the metal showing under the tear. And the petals were starting to go brown. Then it stayed there forever like that, never changing. The paintings were immaculate, but the subjects of the paintings were always worn, broken, about to rot.

He would have thought if you wanted to freeze something in time you'd pick the best possible version of whatever it was. Stunning flowers in a crystal vase, something exotic and expensive, not a handful of wilting blooms somebody cut off the bushes out front. He asked Lane about it once. It was after one of her great parties, early on, and she was in a good mood, a little drunk and happy.

"Who gives a fuck about beauty?" she'd said. "What counts is what's real. We're ugly and we're gonna die. That's what I paint."

"Fuck me," Oliver said, taken aback. "That's a cheerful thought."

She started to laugh. She used to laugh back then. "God, you're young, aren't you. Okay, how's this then: We are beautiful and we'll live forever. You like that better? You like lies?"

"Yes, lie to me."

"You believe that, you're doomed," she said.

"You're loony," he said. "But you're a decent painter."

Lane's decline had been so gradual that he did not always grasp the extent of it. It was only when he thought about the way she was back then that he realized how far gone she was now. Gone, not coming back. He was nearly thirty years old and all he'd done was take care of sick old ladies. His gran, his auntie, now Lane. He'd let it go too far. Should have got her to the doctor before now.

CHAPTER 28

Artie and Marisol packed the girls and the puppy in the back of the car and drove to Wednesday night dinner at his mom's place. It was a family tradition he remembered from childhood, all the cousins, aunts, and uncles would gather at his grandmother's house in Broadmoor. There were fifteen cousins in his generation and everybody lived nearby. Now the whole family was scattered, it was just his older sister still in town with her two kids. And his father's absence left everything diminished.

They parked and the girls started to squabble about which one of them would hold the dog's leash on the way to the door. Marisol unbuckled Pearl from her car seat and lifted her out.

"I'm walking Boudin. It's my turn," she said.

Pearl had always been a quiet baby, none of that baby talk and babble that Colette had done. They had worried about her hearing, her development, but then she'd started speaking in complete grammatical sentences suddenly, a few weeks ago. It still startled them to hear her confident little voice.

"No," Colette said, "I said it first."

Marisol glanced at Art. It was essential to avoid a meltdown in front of his mom. They worried about her. Since Bertrand's death she seemed like she could splinter at any moment.

"Hey, how about we all hold the leash," Artie said.

"No," the girls said.

"I wonder what Boudin would like," Artie said. "Did anyone ask him?"

Pearl grabbed at the puppy's face, managed to brush an ear. "Daddy, he won't talk to me," she said.

Artie lifted the dog in his arms and said, "Boudin, what do you think if we all walk you to the door?" He put his ear to the dog's snout. Boudin licked the side of his face happily. "Really?" Artie said to the dog. "You sure? You got it, bud."

He set the dog down. "He told me he's *very* into this idea. Girls, what do you say?"

"Okay," Colette said.

Pearl had already stationed herself next to the dog, her chubby fist around the leash near his collar. "Daddy, he wants us to," she explained. "He told me, too."

"Okay, Mari, get over here," he said.

The adults had to hunch over to reach the leash, and the four of them shuffled along, forced to go at Pearl's two-year-old pace. The girls were both giggling and talking to the dog. At the door Artie straightened up and opened it. Inside he let the dog off the leash. The girls bounced after him into the house. Artie returned to the car to get the wine and salad they had brought. Back inside he found his mom alone in the kitchen.

"There you are, baby," his mother said.

She had made her butter beans with shrimp, and the smell pervaded the kitchen.

"Hi, Mama," he said. "What can I do?"

"Check on that rice cooker for me, will you? I think it's done."

He lifted the lid. "Yeah, it's done."

"Let's set the table."

Artie opened the silverware drawer. "How many are we tonight?"

"Nine, Joanie couldn't come. She's got play practice or something." His mother took the forks and knives from her son. "How you holding up, babe?"

"I'm fine, Mom."

"Yeah? You can talk to me, you know. Campaigns are hard. Especially the first one. Even if they go well, it's draining for everybody."

"Did Mari say something to you?" he said. Maybe he hadn't been hiding his stress as well as he thought.

"No, no, she hasn't. And she seems great. The girls, too. Such little munchkins. It's you I'm worried about."

"Me? Don't worry about me. I'm doing well in the polls."

"Yes, you'll win this one," she said. "I'm not concerned about that. I know how dirty it can get out there, that's all."

"What do you mean?" he said.

"Honey, I've been through it. Those jackals will dig up anything they can."

"There's nothing to dig up," he said.

She studied his face a moment, the spoon in her hand dripping gravy to the floor. She nodded.

"Good. But if you ever need somebody to help navigate it, you can ask me. I learned a lot from watching your father, you know."

"Mom. I'm not running that kind of campaign," Artie said.

"Oh, honey. I've heard your talking points. But there's how you run, and there's how things work. There has to be *some* overlap."

"I'm fine," Artie said.

She patted her son's cheek. "Remember, you don't have to be perfect. Voters like it when you loosen up."

"Yeah, Mom," he said. "I know."

"You do look tired," she said. "You sleeping enough?"

"Sure," he said. "Almost."

She handed him the stack of plates. "Go set the table."

All through dinner Artie wondered what his mother knew, what she suspected. Neither he nor his dad had ever said a word to her about that night two decades ago. His father could not tell her what really happened, because to reveal it would put her at risk. That's what Bertrand had explained at the time, the promise he'd extracted from his son. *We have to protect your mother and your brother and sisters,* he said. *They can never know.* Later Artie understood that the woman who helped him that night also had to be kept secret from his mother. If he told her, in a moment of weakness, it would destroy his parents' marriage.

There was no reason for his mom to worry. Hadn't he handled the blackmail situation perfectly well by himself? And if they came back at him, he could figure that out, too. He'd be prepared. He'd taken steps already. Shifted some money around. He'd even bought a gun. Not that he planned to use it, but to need one and not have it—well, now he had it.

It's true he'd had trouble sleeping, had added miles to his morning runs to wear his body out, keep himself calm. He'd done the same thing during those first months at boarding school. He had been a different person then, a child. He hadn't yet learned to reinvent himself. When he figured out how to do that, his new life closed around that night and contained it, compressed it, until it took up no space in him at all. It was like the whole thing had happened to someone else and Artie had only heard about it secondhand.

But since that letter came, the past kept creeping around. It showed up in his dreams, the smell of blood and urine and burned rubber, flashes of that night—out of nowhere, a man in the street. The thump, the squeal of the tires as Artie's leg pushes down the pedal. The wrong one, he tries to brake, and in his alarm pushes the accelerator instead. Outside of the car, sitting on the pavement, cradling the man's head in his lap, Artie's arms and legs wet with blood, his face wet with tears. That scene replaying, waking him. He could never get back to sleep after that, even if it was three or four in the morning.

But he would be fine. He took a second helping of beans and bounced Pearl on his lap, making her giggle while he ate.

CHAPTER 29

In the weeks following Oliver's return from New York, he brought Ava presents. Records, an old WWOZ T-shirt, faded and soft from washing, a cute plush pelican that she was too old for but slept with anyway. He'd kept his distance at first, but if she was staying, well then. They talked about Lane.

"I'm counting on you," Oliver said. "I can't be here all the time, so we have to help each other out. Tell me if there's any new freak-outs. Or if she gets to be too much for you. I can come over."

"She hasn't even noticed the stove doesn't work," Ava said.

"Didn't think she would."

Ava thought of her mom, who had cooked dinner almost every night. They ate red beans a lot, and gumbo, but more often a simple stir-fry with tofu and vegetables, or pasta with roasted winter squash and wilted greens. Healthy simple recipes that came from magazines her boss's boss left in the break room at the factory.

"Did Lane used to cook when my mom was little?" Ava asked.

"Jeez, I don't know, how old do you think I am?"

Oliver was high, had been smoking through the afternoon as he went about his errands and chores. He brought the mail in, smoked, tidied up a bit, smoked, sorted through the bills and paid them. Now he was smoking again.

Ava held her hand out for the pipe.

"Fuck, no," Oliver said calmly.

"Why?"

"It'll ruin your brain. Besides, that's not my decision to make."

"I'll just get it from Lane when you're not here," Ava said. "I want to try it."

"Why?"

"Cause she's high all the time. I want to find out what it's like for her."

Oliver peered at Ava. "You are an interesting little human, you know that?"

"I'm not little," she said. "I'm almost as tall as you."

"Smoking dope is not going to teach you what it's like to be Lane," he said. "Nobody's like her. Nobody understands how her brain works."

"You mean what's wrong with her?"

"No. I mean she's different. Always was. She pays more attention to what's inside her head than what's out here."

"I figured that out already."

"You know why, though?"

"Why?"

"Cause it's better. Her thoughts, or whatever they are, are more interesting than what's outside. More complicated. For me it's the opposite. I'd rather be out talking to people, listen to some music, try a new bar, whatever. Cause inside my head it's only me, it's boring. But she's never bored, she doesn't need anything else."

"Then why does she smoke?"

"To help her think. For me, it's the opposite. I can't do shit when I'm high, really. Not anything important."

"Talking to me isn't important?"

"Okay, little girl. You know what I mean. We're just hanging out. But Lane goes right to work."

"Why do you smoke?"

"Cause it's here, I guess. I started too young, I get bored without it. Makes the boring shit less boring. Plus it's free."

"What do you mean it's free?"

"Well, it's not my money. It's a perk of the job. Give me a break, girl."

"I'll give you a break if you give me some."

"You're killing me."

"Fine. I'll stare at you until you let me."

Ava opened her eyes wide and looked into Oliver's, cataloging their shape, their golden flecks within the gray-hazel irises. She noted a faint white line bisecting his right brow.

"What's that scar from?" she said.

"Got punched in the face when I was a kid," he said.

"Why?"

"People are dicks, what do you mean why?"

"That's sad."

"Quit looking at me."

"Let me smoke, then."

"God, this is unnerving," he said.

"I'm happy to stop anytime."

Ava barely cared about the pot. But she was curious to see what she could get away with, how easily Oliver would bend to pressure.

"You're too young," he said. "Your brain is still whatever. Still forming."

"Grown-ups always say that."

"It's true. If you want to get high so bad, why haven't you stolen some off Lane already?"

"I'm a good kid."

"Yeah. I fucking noticed."

"Also . . ." Ava finally broke eye contact.

"Also what?"

"She thinks I'm my mom."

"Fuck. Really?"

"You've heard her call me Louise, haven't you?"

"She gets names mixed up, that doesn't mean anything."

"She never calls *you* a different name. I think she's mad at me. Or afraid of me, maybe? I didn't even do anything."

"She and your mom didn't get along too well, I guess. Y'all never came down here."

"My mom talked about New Orleans, though. She missed it a lot."

"Must be weird for you," Oliver said. He did feel sorry for her.

"Sometimes it's like she doesn't know I'm here. And the rest of the time it seems like she hates me."

"She doesn't hate you. That's just how she is, these days. She wasn't always like that. She used to be more fun. More on top of things."

Lane had been funny, hyperobservant, quick. She hadn't been funny in a long while. She'd lost that and it probably wasn't coming back. It was depressing to think about.

"How about some ice cream?" he said.

"What kind do we have?"

"Blue Bell. Mint chocolate chip."

"Okay," Ava said.

Ava was glad Oliver hadn't given in. It was nice to have

somebody watching out for her. They ate on the narrow balcony, surveying the roofs of garages in the alleyway. When they had finished, Oliver took the empty bowls to the kitchen and left. He could tell Ava was hoping he'd stay later. It was lonely for the kid. Lane wasn't great company these days, and now that she'd begun her new piece, they barely saw her.

The next morning Ava was sipping iced coffee when Oliver banged through the front door. She went to meet him.

"Morning, Little Bit," he said. "What's shaking?"

"Lane's not up yet."

"Cool. Let's see what she did yesterday. Come on."

Ava followed him into the front room. She was about to ask him if he'd called Kaitlyn yet, or talked to Lane about her situation. But she forgot all that when she saw the drawing.

Lane's sketch covered the entire wall. She had roughed in a landscape, the sea in the background, and a figure, a child, standing on the beach. Straggly grasses and palmettos protruding from the sand, cloud shapes, boats, a crushed beer can washed up onshore. Sandcastles, the remains of a bonfire, and the girl, facing Ava, her back to the sea, holding a crawfish, showing it off. The girl was unmistakably Louise.

"Coming along," Oliver said. "It'll be pretty. She got a lot done yesterday. Must have been up late."

Ava half-heard. She walked forward to stand in front of the girl, perhaps seven or eight years old. The little girl's hand extended toward Ava. She was sketched lines, she was pencil on a wall. But she was Ava's mother and she was coming to life. Her face more excited than afraid of the crawfish's snapping pincers, her posture, the part of her hair, the ties of her little sundress at her shoulders flapping in the sea wind. It was magic: Louise was dead, but here, again, was Louise. Ava began to tremble.

"God, she made a mess of this floor," Oliver said. "Check out these scratches. It's dusty in here, too. It'll have to be cleaned before she starts painting. Some of these chairs could go in the living room for now. I wonder if she's doing more than the one wall. We could shove everything else over there." He picked up one side of the heavy wingback chair Lane had moved the day before. "Ava, hello. Give me a hand."

She turned to face him, unable to speak.

"Aw, girl, now what?" He set the chair down and came to her.

Ava turned back to face the drawing. "It's my mom," she whispered.

Oliver put his arm around her and drew her to him. In his embrace her whole body became a conduit of grief. Sobs wracked her frame. She leaned into him, she clutched at his shirt, now soaked with tears. Her occasional hiccups and labored breathing were the only sounds. He held her until she calmed down.

Finally she let go of Oliver, came back to herself, and turned away, embarrassed.

"Okeydoke," he said. "Take a shower, get dressed, get yourself together. You're coming with me. Go on."

She obeyed, stood under the hot water until she felt stronger, then dressed in her favorite shorts and old Iowa Hawkeyes shirt. She brushed her hair and stepped into her sneakers.

He drove them up Magazine through the park, to a riverside cottage turned into a bakery. He ordered for her: crawfish baguette, iced mocha, an almond croissant.

"This oughta fix you up, Little Bit," he said. "Carbs always do the trick."

Ava ate and began to feel more present, less depleted. They sat in the front window and beheld the narrow, rutted street and the levee wall beyond it. Gulls lined up atop the wall, squawking and messy, swooping down to pick at trash in the gutter. Ava thought of the pelican on the front room wall.

"How long will it take her to finish the painting?" she asked.

"A couple weeks, maybe a month if she gets distracted."

"She has to finish it."

"She will."

"When school starts, I'll be gone during the day."

"You worry too much," Oliver said. "She'll be fine, I'm gonna be there. Just like I was before you came to town."

Ava pushed the remains of her breakfast toward Oliver. "I'm full," she said.

"Well, I'm not eating it," he said. "You trying to get me fat?" He got a go-box for the leftovers and drove her home.

CHAPTER 30

Since her last conversation with Kaitlyn, Ava had started checking the mail every day. The mail lady came in the early afternoons with utility bills and flyers and credit card offers, but no packages from Iowa City. Ava tossed out the junk and piled the rest on the front table for Oliver to go through.

One afternoon Ava returned from a sweaty bike ride through the park. She heard Lane muttering to herself in the front room and peeked in.

"Need any help?" Ava said.

"No," Lane said.

"Did the mail come?"

Lane straightened up and glared at Ava. "I'm busy," Lane said.

"Sorry." Ava backed away.

In the kitchen she found evidence that Oliver had been there: some Costco bags of toilet paper, peanut butter and other sundries, and a Styrofoam container of shrimp salad in the fridge. Ava poured a glass of water and went searching for the mail. She found a pile of papers on top of Lane's desk in the studio, under a heavy pink shell Lane used as a paperweight. Ava went through the pile, looking for the package from Kaitlyn. Oliver had opened the envelopes and unfolded their contents. A utility bill, a bill from an accountant, a credit card bill, a notice from a car insurance company. Nothing for Ava. She started to put the papers back where she'd found them when something caught her eye. She examined the credit card bill more carefully.

The balance was over $5,000. Louise had kept a credit card for emergencies. She taught Ava about it, how dangerous it was to let the debt pile up. Ava remembered the day they had paid off their balance after they'd used it to fix the car. It took six months to pay off the $600 charge at the mechanic, and they'd ended up paying more because of interest. Louise had explained that it was worth it because without the car she couldn't drive to work, and the bus didn't run for the early shift, so she would have lost her job or spent even more money on cabs. How much of this was interest and late fees? How long had it gone on?

Ava checked the previous balance and payments and saw that Oliver had paid the last month's bill in full, but it was high, too: $4,300. Could New Orleans be that expensive? Sure, they ate out a lot, but she'd seen the price of takeout lunches, and it did not explain this.

Ava read through the charges. She recognized some restaurants, the drugstore, the grocery, the post office and bookstore and art supply shop. There were a bunch of charges for places in New Orleans she wasn't familiar with. And then there were some in New York—cabs, restaurants, theater tickets. Why had Lane paid for this stuff? It was so much money.

Ava had to ask Lane. There must be an explanation other than the one that clearly suggested itself. She carried the bill to the front room, where Lane stood, staring at the blank white expanse to the left of the mantel.

"Lane."

Lane kept her eyes on the blank wall, concentrating.

"Lane, I have to show you something," Ava said.

"Oh, for god's sake, I'm working!" Lane turned toward Ava, truly angry. "Out, get out!" She threw the pencil she was holding in Ava's direction and Ava fled.

Outside, away from Lane, Ava tried to think. Maybe Lane agreed to pay for Oliver's trip. Maybe he was buying things for her in New York. It was possible, she supposed.

Ava took her bike along the riverbend and back, to the trail at Audubon Park. She sat in the grass and watched people feed bread to the ducks. The ducks fought over the crumbs, and the more aggressive ones waddled up onshore among the tree roots and spread their wings, menacing. A toddler holding a bread sack started to bawl and his mother scooped him up and shoved the duck away with her foot.

What if Oliver was stealing? She hoped he wasn't, but if he was, what did it mean? He cared about Lane, loved her, Ava could tell. What kind of person was he, anyway? She read the Visa card statement again. She had to bring it to Lane, to wait for the right moment. But it needed to be soon. For all she knew, Oliver was out right now buying himself more presents.

A new thought occurred to her—the candlesticks, the silver, other objects that had gone missing. Maybe Oliver had taken those, too. Lane certainly didn't remember sending them to get appraised. Maybe she had, it was possible. But Ava saw how easy it would be for him to take things. How often she'd seen Oliver carrying bags and boxes out to his car. She'd assumed he was doing something for Lane, she had never questioned what was in them. All the times she'd seen him rooting around in the pantry, the closets, the backs of cabinets. When Lane was painting, she didn't notice anything else. You could stand on your head in a clown suit and Lane wouldn't even look up.

Back at the house Ava found Lane still working. She sat reading a book in the living room, where she could listen for her. Finally she heard her grandmother come out.

"Lane," Ava said. "Lane. I need to talk to you."

"I need coffee," Lane said.

Ava followed her to the kitchen.

"It's about Oliver," Ava said.

"What?"

"I found this." Ava held out the credit card statement.

Lane glanced at it. "So? Give it to Oliver, that's his job." She sat at the table and lit her pipe.

"Can you please put that down and listen? This is really important. There's all these charges for his vacation, and other stuff, too. It's a lot of money. Did you say he could do this?"

Lane shrugged.

"I think he's using your credit card to buy things for himself."

"That's his job," Lane said. "He does the shopping, the bills. He's supposed to."

"I know. But I think. . . ."

"I don't have time for this."

"Listen," Ava said. She read the names of boutiques, bars, the MoMA gift shop. She checked to see if Lane was understanding. Lane nodded politely, without expression.

"I think he is taking advantage of you. Stealing. Maybe taking things, too. Antiques."

This got Lane's attention. "What antiques?" she said.

"Remember the candlesticks we searched everywhere for? The silver candlesticks with the grapes? They belonged to your . . . your uncle, maybe?"

"Where are they?"

"They're in the pantry, I got them back for you. But I found them in Oliver's car."

"Why were they in Oliver's car?"

"He said he was getting them appraised."

"Well, that makes sense," Lane said.

"Well," Ava said. "If he was telling the truth."

"Why would he lie about that?"

"Lane, you're always saying how valuable these things are. Oliver might have sold them and kept the money."

"This is ridiculous."

"Please read the bill? Please?"

"Fine, give it here."

Lane grabbed the pages from Ava and skimmed them. She recognized some of the places—bars, restaurants in Oliver's neighborhood, Red's Chinese and Saba, places she never went. The girl, the Louise lookalike, sat and watched her.

"Where's Oliver?" Lane asked.

"I don't know. He's not here."

"We need to straighten out this problem, this is why I have him. So I don't have to . . ."

Her voice trailed away. Something wasn't right about the situation. Something was off. Her mind worked its way around, like picking up stones along a path. She didn't know which stones she needed, if it was even a stone she was looking for. The afternoon light streamed in, illuminating dust mites in the air. Oliver was supposed to arrange for a cleaner and he still hadn't done it.

"Lane," the girl said. "He wasn't supposed to do this, was he?"

"I don't think so," Lane said.

"He's been stealing from you. Taking advantage of you."

"What do you want me to do?" Lane said. "Fire him? Oliver does everything."

"I can help you," Ava said. "I can do some of it, and we can find somebody else. It will be okay."

"We can't find somebody else."

"We'll figure it out," Ava said. "We can get things delivered. I have my bike, and you can drive places when we need to."

"No," Lane said. "No, no, no."

"But you can't let him stay. You can't trust him."

"How much did he take?"

"I'm not sure. I don't know how long it's been happening."

Lane picked up her pipe.

Ava frowned. "Have you eaten anything today?"

"Of course."

"Really? What did you have?"

"Some leftovers. Some toast, I think."

Ava doubted this was true. "I'm going to fix us something." She patted Lane awkwardly on the shoulder.

Lane shrugged off her touch. It was like the girl was trying to impose a sense of order that did not actually exist. She was operating from a set of false assumptions. Or maybe people's lives really were moral and tidy in wherever the hell she was from. Iowa.

Lane lit her pipe, smoked, thought. Oliver, Oliver. He was the person she would ask to handle a situation like this. Anger surged through her. What a waste. A waste of time, the most precious, most valuable thing. She wondered how many hours this would set her back. Why did a person have to need other people? Lane stood, paced, sat down to study the bill. She turned to a fresh page in her sketchbook and wrote, *Oliver is stealing from me. Using credit card. Selling antiques. How long?* After a moment she added the date.

She stood again. She couldn't hold still. She left the girl in the kitchen and went to the front of the house, back to the painting on the wall, something she could look at that made sense.

This room. Louise in here on summer mornings, reading on the sofa, staring out the window at the street below. Stretched on the floor with blocks, with coloring books. The leaded diamond pattern in the old front windows casting shadows on her bare foot, one leg stretched out on the sofa, the other bent beneath her. There was no place in this house that belonged to Lane alone. It was crammed with old iterations. Louise at fifteen, disdainful, next to a Christmas tree. Lane had quit that holiday decorating nonsense when Louise left, and now she wished she'd kept it up, kept doing everything. She should have gone to visit Louise. Should have put in that effort. Tried harder. She read the sentences in the sketchbook. Oliver. Her despair outweighed her, she thought she might collapse.

"Lane. Come on, I fixed you a plate."

Lane startled at the voice. The not-Louise, the fake one. The new one, standing in the doorway on spindly legs. Where was her real daughter? This was not the right question, Lane sensed. The right questions were gone, hidden somewhere. The girl was tall but still a child. Lane followed her to the kitchen, sat down. Ate the food on the plate without tasting it.

"What are you going to do?" Ava asked.

"I don't know," Lane said.

"I mean, maybe you could call him? Tell him to come here? You'll have to get your credit card back. Or it might be better to cancel it, get a new one."

"I suppose so. Let me think about it."

Ava fidgeted. "If you think about it," she said finally, "you might forget. You *are* going to fire him, right?"

"That's enough," Lane said. "I'm not helpless. I've kept all of this shit going, I've taken care of everything, I've done it on my own since before you were born. Since before your mother was born. Quit talking to me like you're scared of me, I can't stand it."

"I'm sorry," Ava said.

"Stop apologizing. Go somewhere else, alright?"

Ava stood and backed away from the table. In a minute Lane heard her go out the door. Finally. She returned to the front room, back to the painting, the only thing left that mattered.

CHAPTER 31

Oliver pulled up in front of the house around ten the next morning. He'd spent the previous night tracking down weed for Lane. He'd had to go three deep into his backup dealers, because it was summer. Everyone was on vacation, the city was hot and slow, nobody was returning calls. He'd finally lucked out with a friend of a friend who'd come back from California with a pound of pure sativa.

It had turned into one of those nights, getting blasted with a stranger and wandering the neighborhood. He'd run into a girl he used to know back in high school, they'd been baristas together at CC's. She was coming out of a play in that little community theater on St. Claude and they ended up having a drink. The girl was with her cousin, an out-of-towner from Dallas or somewhere. He'd walked with them over to Frenchmen to go hear music. The club was jammed with tourists even in July. The band was proficient but their funk songs went on too long. The repetitive rhythm got in Oliver's head and bored him so intensely that he thought for a moment he might actually cry. The music was like the world ending.

He took his drink outside and wound up in a conversation

on the sidewalk with the guy who had tried to shut down the St. Roch Market when it had first reopened. The guy was still mad about it, drunk and belligerent, talking *gentrification this, food desert that*. "Don't blame me," Oliver remembered saying, "I'm up above St. Claude." But the truth was he'd eaten there plenty, with John and his posh friends, and the food was no shit amazing. He smoked some more of the weed with the guy and couldn't remember everything after that, but it was past four when he made it home.

The weed was still fucking with him a little in the morning, he woke up too early, twitchy and irritable. He was in no mood for Ava's little face frowning at him on Lane's porch.

"Morning," Oliver said.

"You should go," Ava said. "Wait for Lane to call you."

"Why in the fuck would I do that? What's going on?"

"She's still sleeping. She worked late last night."

"So did I," Oliver said.

"Please wait and talk to Lane."

"I'm coming in, I need a coffee."

Ava stood in the doorway, blocking his way.

"Iowa, I'm not in the mood for any bullshit. Move."

"Come back later."

"No. What's with you?"

He put his hands on her spiky shoulders and forcibly shifted her to the side. In the house he went back to the kitchen, fixed himself iced coffee, and found some aspirins in the cabinet. Lane's pipe was on the kitchen table, with a bit left in the bowl. He smoked it. In a few minutes he'd feel well enough to pick up lunch. Something with cheese melted on it.

From his pocket he pulled the bag of weed he'd bought and set it on the table. The kid had followed him through and stood there scowling.

"What's with you, grumpyface?" he said.

"Oliver, you should really go."

"Did something happen? Is Lane okay?" His stomach tensed. He'd never seen Ava act like this. He refilled the bowl with the new sativa, for something to do with his hands.

"No, she's not okay. Oliver, I've seen the credit card bill. I know you've been using it for yourself. And taking stuff, too. Those candlesticks. You were going to sell them, weren't you? What else have you stolen? Did you take that silverware, too?"

Oliver laughed. Took a hit off the pipe, why not? The moment was already surreal, beyond belief.

"It's not funny," Ava said. "I'm serious, you can't be here anymore."

"I get it," he said. "Little farm girl is pretending to fire me. Cute."

"Oliver, I have proof. She could bring charges against you. You could go to jail."

"Are you crazy?" he said. "You're going to call the cops? Who do you think is going to jail?" He tossed the bag of weed to Ava. She let it bounce off her and fall to the floor. "This is enough for intent to distribute. How you think she'd do in prison? Think she'd adjust to that pretty well? Or maybe they'd put her in with the crazies, once they figure out she can't remember shit."

"Oliver, please," Ava said. She was starting to sniffle, trying not to show it. "Please go."

"She needs me," he said. "She'll fall apart without me."

"She needs someone she can trust," Ava said.

"No. She needs *me*."

"I can take care of her."

"You?" Oliver laughed again. "Be serious."

Ava sat at the table, depleted. She let the tears run down her face.

"Shit," he said. "Don't cry. Come on." He got up, fixed her a coffee and handed it to her. He took another hit off the pipe. His thoughts were going too fast, and he struggled to focus.

"Ava," he said, sitting down. "You need to think about this. Think it through. You want what's best for Lane. I know you do."

Ava nodded.

"Good. Believe it or not, so do I. You're right, I shouldn't have spent that money. That was a mistake. I was wrong to do that. And I won't do it again."

Ava shook her head.

"Listen to me," Oliver said. "You've been here for what? Two months? Not even. You don't know shit about her. Or this town. Or anything. You didn't know her before. What she was like. I've been taking care of your grandmother for almost ten years. Since before you even started kindergarten, probably. I know her, I know what she needs."

"We can find someone else," Ava said.

"Sure. Sure you can. And how long will that take? To find somebody who won't mind the way she treats people, who will put up with her temper? It took me a year to learn this job, to get the hang of it. Her yelling at me almost every single day. I don't know a single person who would put up with that. And that was before."

"Before what?" Ava said dully.

"Before she started to forget things. Bring in a new person, it's not going to go well. She needs, what's it called? Consistency."

"How much did you take, Oliver? How long's it been going on?"

"You're not listening to me, are you? That's not the point. Nobody cares about her more than me. Think it through."

"You have to leave," Ava said. "And don't come back."

"You think Lane cares about money? You don't understand her at all."

"She cares about trust."

"Maybe." Oliver shrugged. "Maybe you have no idea what she cares about. I do."

"Wait and see what she says."

"It's done, it's over. I promise you she won't notice that, either. Or care. Just, please, keep it between us."

"I can't."

"Don't tell her. I get that you love her, she's your family. You're a really good person, you care about right and wrong. What I did was wrong. I admit that. But think of what would truly be best for Lane. The stress this would cause, the disruption."

"You should have thought of that when you decided to steal."

"Please, Ava. Don't tell her."

"It's too late," Ava said. "She already knows."

Oliver rose from his seat, slowly, as if his body was some jerky puppet, controlled by distant forces. *Don't hit her,* he thought. *Don't hit her don't hit her don't hit her.* He leaned over the table with its stack of newspapers and mail, the two plastic Mardi Gras cups of milky coffee and ice. In a single swipe of his arm he sent it to the floor. They both watched the coffee spread over the hardwoods, the oblongs of ice skitter and bounce off the baseboards.

"You have no idea what you've done," Oliver said.

He left the room. Ava heard the front door open and slam, rattling the glass in the windows. She retrieved the cups and the mail, now wet with coffee. She picked up the ice cubes and lay towels down to soak up the spill.

As Ava cleaned, doubt consumed her thoughts. Had she made a mistake? What would happen to Lane without Oliver? What had she done? She spread the mail on dish towels and blotted it dry, then wiped down the baseboards and walls and table legs with a wet rag. She wiped coffee from the plastic bag of marijuana and set it back on the table. We'll be okay, she said to herself, but she didn't believe it.

Lane appeared in the doorway, shuffling, the sleepy-eyed morning look on her face.

"Hi," Ava said. "I'll get you some coffee." She made a cup and handed it to Lane.

"Thanks," Lane said. "Why is this wet?" She gestured at the mail, the newspaper laid out on towels.

"Oliver spilled—" She paused because she heard the front door open and close. Lane was trying to read the wet newspaper. Ava listened to Oliver's footsteps in the hall. He came into the kitchen as if nothing had happened, carrying three pink bakery boxes.

"Almond croissants," he announced cheerfully. "And sandwiches for later. I went to O'Delice, they do better pastries than Boulangerie now. Wait til you try this sandwich. Ham and Gruyere with slices of cold butter, holy shit. Ava, you'll love it."

Ava glared at him. Lane sipped her coffee. Oliver put a croissant on a plate and set it on the table, watched Lane pick it up and take a bite. He pulled the wooden pipe from his pocket.

"Accidentally took this with me," he said. "Sorry." He handed it to Lane with a lighter. "Go a little easy at first, with this stuff. It can mess with your head."

Lane smoked. Oliver sat with her at the table, ignoring Ava.

"Lane," Ava said. "You have to . . . do you remember what we talked about yesterday?"

Lane squinted at her through the smoke. "God," she said. "I just woke up. Give me a break, alright."

"Sorry," Ava mumbled, her eyes welling again. She left the room, sick of crying in front of them.

She wished she could leave, get as far away as possible. She considered going back to Iowa. She could ask Lane to buy her a plane ticket. Kaitlyn could pick her up from the airport in Cedar Rapids. Or she could go on the bus. The Greyhound would take her right into Iowa City and she could walk to her old apartment. She let herself visualize it, the trail along the river that wound through downtown and the university campus, the Old Capitol building with its gold dome and green lawn sloping away. She could stay with Kaitlyn and her new roommate, or with friends from school, or even live with the crusty kids who asked for change on the Ped Mall. She could start City High in the fall. Leave Lane and Oliver together. They were both adults. She was the child. Why shouldn't she leave?

But she couldn't stand the idea of Oliver alone with Lane, no one to protect her. Ava waited on the front porch, paced down and up the steps. She went out front and sat on Oliver's car, but the hood burned her bare thighs and she hopped off.

Oliver's leg was jiggling the table, sending rings over the surface of Lane's coffee.

"Can't you hold still?" Lane said.

"Sorry. It's the weed. And not enough sleep, I guess."

"You need to get a cleaner in here."

Oliver groaned. "Shit, I forgot. Been meaning to. I'll call them right now."

"It really needs it. Dust everywhere. But keep them out of the front room."

"Okay, I'll arrange it. But remember what happened last time. Try not to yell at them, okay?"

"Well, tell them not to mess with my stuff," Lane said. "That's your responsibility."

"Yeah, yeah. And you'll have to hide the weed."

"Just get them in here." She studied the pipe. "This shit is zingy."

"Thought you'd like it," he said.

Lane stood and fixed a second cup of coffee.

"Hey, I checked out the painting," he said. "That's Ava's mom? It's gonna be gorgeous."

"We'll see." Lane had a superstitious aversion to talking about a piece before it was finished.

"That kid is something else. Can't imagine what her mother was like."

Lane shrugged. "She was too good for me. She up and left. It took me forever to figure out where she was, even. I had to hire someone to find her."

"Like a detective?"

"Yeah. I hated to think of her, trapped on a farm, those terrible winters, so goddamn young, no high school diploma."

"God, that sounds depressing," Oliver said.

"Nothing I could do. She was eighteen. Wouldn't listen to me. I wrote her letters, sent money. Checks she never even cashed. I never heard a thing until Ava was born."

"Jeez. Stubborn."

"She was, yeah."

"Sounds like you, a little."

"Oh, come on. She wasn't anything like me. She was prissy, very responsible. When she was ten years old she threatened to call the cops over my dope."

"Shit. Even Ava wouldn't pull a stunt like that."

"God, why are we talking about Louise? Let's talk about something else."

"You're the one obsessed with her."

"What?"

"The painting."

"I can't talk about the painting."

"Fine, whatever."

"I've got to get started. Don't forget about the cleaner."

"Lane," Oliver said.

"What?" she was impatient now, ready to work.

"Listen, whatever happens, I'll always look out for you, alright? Whether you want me to or not. I'm not going anywhere."

"Yeah, sure," Lane said. She was already halfway down the hall.

He followed her to the front of the house and peered through the window. The kid was still hanging around, leaning on his car. He called goodbye to Lane and went outside to face Ava.

"I'm leaving," he said. "But I'm coming back. She needs me."

Ava shook her head.

"So do you," he said.

"I'll be fine," she said. "Just go."

"Then get your ass off my car."

Ava backed away and watched him get in, turn the key, put his seat belt on. She was still standing there. He could see her in the rearview mirror as he turned the corner.

CHAPTER 32

Oliver felt stunned. Exhausted. On the ride home a calm stole over him. He had to blink to stay awake. How peculiar, how odd. If he'd ever let himself imagine this moment, he would have thought that he'd lose his shit. But here he was, calmly driving through the neighborhood, practically falling asleep at the wheel. He rolled the windows down and let the hot wet wind blow through the car, keeping him awake. He parked outside his place, ignoring the yelling crackhead who lived two doors down, always on the front porch trying to start drama. The block wasn't bad except for that guy. Oliver let himself in and collapsed into bed and troubled dreams.

It was dark out when he woke. He walked a couple of blocks to the laundromat dive bar, sat in front of a pick-3 machine, and proceeded to get as fucked up as possible. Bourbon after bourbon in thin plastic cups.

He felt violated, thinking of Ava with that credit card statement. His spending was not something he was proud of, and it wasn't her business, anyway. He was stupid with money, he blew it on insignificant things—nights out, sunglasses, fucking New York City.

He'd overdone it in New York. But he'd wanted to impress John, to treat him, to experience a terrific vacation for once—Broadway, nice dinners. He'd wanted to feel like he could belong in a place like that, with its cosmopolitan sophistication, art, fashion. He'd known his whole life what it was like to be looked down on, dismissed—sketchy little coonass, drug dealer, poor white boy, queer. He thought maybe New York would be big enough, full of enough strangers who wouldn't care where he'd come from.

The problem was nobody there saw him at all. And the buildings crowded him, he had that pounding in his chest, his shoulders tensed up and stayed that way until he got off the plane at Louis Armstrong Airport. Even the Broadway musical, he didn't much care for. The music got on his nerves, and the audience was mostly tourists, fat Midwesterners in horrible churchy clothes.

The city was so dirty. They spent a lot on cabs because the subway made him claustrophobic and paranoid. Oliver was disappointed with himself for not liking it better, for not being more adventurous. He responded to his anxiety by shopping. New scarf, new shoes.

He could practically hear his auntie—if she were here, she'd tell him, You don't need that nonsense. Maybe she was right, but ever since grade school, Oliver always longed for things they couldn't afford. He had an eye, too. He knew he did. He had good taste, a sense of aesthetics. If he had Lane's house, he would make it shine. He wouldn't even need to buy anything new, he would just get rid of two-thirds of what was in there, edit it down to the best pieces, repaint. She had too much and didn't care about it. Why shouldn't Oliver help himself?

The first time he took something was four years ago. It was almost like she wanted him to. She'd become fixated on the antiques that were crammed in every cabinet—she would empty out an entire closet of stuff. Old tea urns, linens, framed portraits, bookends, ancient fancy hats with rotting lace and feathers.

"All this garbage, all these *things*," she said in disgust. "This house is full of poison." She picked up one of the hats, an origami-folded amalgamation of wool felt and silk flowers. "This was Bitsy's," Lane said. "Papa's favorite aunt. Bitsy had hats coming out of her ass." Lane tossed it onto the bed, piled high with assorted junk. "You can't get away from 'em. Even when they're dead."

Oliver beheld the mess, every surface covered in crap from the closet. He was irritated because he would have to clean it up before she went to bed that night, and he already had an afternoon's worth of errands. He figured the painting wasn't going well. She got into these moods. She never thought about anybody but herself. He'd been kicking around the idea of asking for a raise.

"Did you need the closet for something?" he asked her. "Do you need the space?"

He could box the stuff up and haul it downstairs, where it could get ruined in the soggy basement. Or drop it at Goodwill. Or he could cram it back where she'd pulled it from.

"I don't need the closet. For what, more garbage?" She sat down on the edge of the bed and loaded her pipe.

"How's the work coming along?" Oliver said.

"The work. It's great, can't you tell?" She gestured around at the disorder of the room, smoke drifting out of her nostrils. "How's the work, Jesus."

She handed him the lit bowl. "I should get back to it. Could you—?"

"Yeah, yeah, I'll clean it up, don't worry. But I won't have time to get out to the campus today." He was supposed to pick up some copies of blueprints from Tulane's architecture library, and he couldn't stay late, he had dinner plans.

A teetering pile of linens fell off the bed when Lane stood up. She kicked it under. "I'm sick of this shit. Other people's memories. Some of it is valuable, you know."

Back then he knew nothing of antiques, but he took note of what was there, and stacked it neatly on the closet shelves. He didn't do anything about it right away, but it happened that a couple of weeks later, on his day off, he met John, who turned out to be the owner of a reputable antiques shop on Magazine. It was like the universe put the idea in his head and Oliver was obligated to respond, to follow this path and see where it led.

Oliver never exactly lied about the items he put on consignment in John's store. It began with the silver-plated tea urn, a heavy object, hideous and large. "It belongs to my boss," he said. "She's trying to clean out her closets." It was true, sort of, and John assumed Oliver was giving Lane the money. At times Oliver really did think he was helping Lane. She hardly ever noticed anything missing, and he was reducing the clutter in her house, little by little. He found a way to compensate himself for the bullshit he had to put up with from her. The tantrums, the inconsistencies. Some months he pocketed an extra hundred or two. Some months, a thousand, occasionally more. The objects came from the deepest recesses of the closets and cupboards. The stealing, if you chose to call it that, which Oliver didn't, was an action with no consequences.

One night Oliver was home making gumbo. Lane called to bitch at him because she couldn't find some book he'd gotten for her. After yelling at him for ten minutes she found it in the dining room, where Oliver had told her to look in the first place. She didn't even apologize, let alone thank him. Just hung up the phone without even saying goodbye. Oliver slammed the kitchen cabinet shut in frustration, and the cheap particleboard door broke off and fell onto the pile of chopped onion and peppers. Oliver left it there and walked up the street to the bar, abandoning his dinner to the roaches.

He charged his tab to Lane's credit card. He knew what she had in her bank account, and she never opened the bills. All she did was make trouble for him, get high and rant and expect him to clean up her messes. She could buy him a night out every now and then. It was impossible for Oliver to feel bad about what he did.

Ava had no understanding of money, or Lane, or how anything worked. Now, three whiskeys in, a rage burst forth toward the girl, for knowing. Little bitch, he thought. Nosy. She had ruined everything.

The thing was, and he didn't know for sure, but he thought maybe, before Ava came around, that when Lane died—not that he was looking forward to that, he really wasn't, he loved Lane, and losing her would devastate him. But the thing was, he really thought that when she passed, she might leave him something. Not the whole estate or anything like that, but some of it, enough to make a significant difference to Oliver. She never said as much, not exactly, but he had understood the daughter had been out of the picture for years. The granddaughter, he didn't even *know* about—that's how estranged they were. Lane didn't give a shit about charity, or community, or anything like that. He didn't see her leaving her money to a homeless shelter or even an art museum. He knew how much she made, and it was plenty. She didn't even need it. Didn't spend it. There was money in a fund, old Domino Sugar money, left over from a couple generations back. It had kept her in the house, sent her daughter to

Newman back in the day, it bought paints, gave her the time to make art. The way he saw it, he was spending money that would eventually be his anyway.

By his fifth drink his anger flattened into remorse. He couldn't be mad at Ava, not really. She was right and he was wrong. She wasn't just right, though. She was *good*. A genuinely good person, despite the shit she'd been through. She'd taken a blow, her mom dying. Poor Ava. And then her only living relative turned out to be Lane, not exactly the nurturing type. Plenty of kids would be afraid of somebody like that, or resentful. But Ava was trying to take care of her, in her way. She was loyal, unselfish. Oliver respected it.

She was young, that's all. And she'd had a wholesome-enough childhood to think right and wrong never overlapped. He wondered if that was an Iowa thing, that innocence she had. That sincerity. He didn't think he'd been so sweet at her age. Maybe not ever.

Oliver needed to walk. He pulled out his wallet to pay the tab, using his own cash. Tomorrow he'd buy a bottle and drink at home to save money. He'd figure out a new plan. He stumbled down the street, tripped over the buckled sidewalk, sloshing his drink. He stopped, propped himself against a tree and drank the rest. He tossed the cup in the gutter and walked on, entered his tiny apartment. The alcohol had done its numbing work, rendered him thickheaded and drowsy. He lay on his bed—soft sheets, high thread count, an ornately carved wooden headboard, a quality queen-size reproduction of an eighteenth-century French piece, the one luxury he had allowed himself. He didn't deserve it. Didn't deserve anything nice. He should give this bed to Ava, he thought, falling into sleep.

Oliver avoided Lane's the next day. If she needed something she could call. He showered, drank a beer, strolled up to the corner place for coffee and eggs. At home he brewed more coffee and smoked a joint. By noon he felt better, weary and high but not too hungover. He watched some old episodes of a show he liked on HGTV, where this tiny blond chick renovated houses in Detroit all by herself. He liked it because she was stronger than she looked, and it was her hometown, and she busted her ass to try to make it better. It would be cool to be able to do something like that. Something meaningful.

He'd meant it when he told Ava he wasn't going anywhere. They needed him, whether the kid liked it or not. He just had to convince her that he could be trusted. He wondered what it would take. On TV the blond chick was explaining how this artist was going to turn a dead tree in front of the house into a sculpture. It sounded like an okay idea, but the end result was hideous. It was still a dead tree, but now with ugly chain saw cuts. They painted a yellow sunflower on it, so dumb. Before the episode was over Oliver knew what he had to do.

He would pay Lane back, everything he'd taken. Say he'd spent a thousand a month. Okay, say two thousand, to be on the safe side, going back four years or so. Jesus, that was already close to a hundred grand. And factor in the pieces he'd sold—maybe he'd gotten around twenty from that over the years. John would have it recorded at the shop, he'd have to check the consignment books. He should pay Lane the antiques' full value, though, not just his cut. He was looking at a hundred and fifty, probably, total. He couldn't believe the amount. What did he have to show for it? Expensive cocktails he couldn't remember, a shitty week in New York, a closet of shirts that were already off trend.

He went for a stroll around the neighborhood to clear his head. How was he going to get that kind of money? He had a few thousand in savings, which he'd thought was a lot until yesterday. He could probably go back to dealing, but he hated

the idea. It was too dangerous, for one thing, and the whole
point was to be there for Lane and the kid. If he ended up in
jail, it would only make everything worse. Same if he started a
different job—he'd be too busy to check in on them if he was
tending bar or working at Best Buy or whatever bullshit gig he
could find short notice. Any job he could get was not the kind
where you could save.

There was always the politician, Guidry. It had come off
perfectly before. Maybe it would again. The guy had this kind
of money, Oliver was sure of that. He could take it out of his
daughters' college funds or his retirement or his fucking campaign donations. People like him could always come up with
money if they had to. And if it didn't work, fine. Oliver would
figure out another plan. Even if it was dealing, he would do it
for Lane.

Over the next few days, he sobered up, thought it through,
went to the shop to check John's consignment records. A hundred and fifty would cover it. He hadn't told John anything about
the nonsense with Ava. Fired by a tween. It was too ridiculous,
too sad. And it would bring up questions about the china and
silver he'd sold through John's shop. John might start to wonder
if she'd ever seen the money. If he began to suspect Oliver—well,
that couldn't happen.

He drove past Lane's, but he saw Ava's bike there, locked up
under the carport, and he kept going, automatically swerving
to avoid the potholes on Coliseum. He wondered what she and
Lane were doing right now. He could just see the two of them,
drifting around each other in the old house. Finally he went
back and waited down the block until Ava left on her bicycle.
With luck he could be in and out before she returned.

He let himself in, said hi to Lane in the front room. She
ignored him. Back in the office he wrote another letter to Guidry

and printed it out, along with an envelope. Before he left he looked around, checked the kitchen and the pantry to see if they had everything they needed. It seemed like they were handling things okay. Ava was keeping the place tidy, there were leftovers in the refrigerator, coffee and milk. He said bye to Lane on his way out, but she was deep in it, merely grunting in response. She'd made serious progress on the mural. It was looser, more expressive than her usual style. He liked it better, he thought.

"How y'all doing?" he said. "Getting along without me?"

Lane grunted in response. He knew better than to engage her when she had a brush in her hand.

"Alrighty, then," he said. "I'll check in later." He let himself out and went to mail the letter.

CHAPTER 33

Ava ordered a new credit card, changed the passwords to Lane's bank account, handled the bills, took out the garbage. She swept and mopped the floors, set out some poison traps for the roaches she'd seen in the pantry. She was even able to buy wine at the corner store, though the last time, when she handed over the money, the guy shook his head, unhappy. She wasn't sure he'd sell to her again. Lane would have to go herself next time. Ava dreaded the day they ran out.

In the evenings Ava rode past the park's stables and the big tree, over the train tracks and down to the river, the stretch locals called the Fly. At night other teens hung out there and drank beer. They showed up on bikes, in cars, on foot, with bottles in brown bags and packs of cigarettes and weed, maybe other stuff, too. They seemed like bad kids by Iowa standards, but maybe down here they were normal. They talked about a bunch of people and places that Ava had never heard of, and she'd shrivel inside while nodding, trying to act like she belonged there. They always asked her where she went to school, and when she said she wasn't from there they usually turned away in disinterest. When Lane ran out of pot, she'd have to ask one of them where they got it. Until then she kept herself apart, gazed steadily at the barge lights across the river.

Lane barely left the front room. She had not spoken a word to Ava in three days. She hadn't changed clothes, either, or showered. She smoked, she wore a loose button-down shirt and some ratty old shorts dotted with paint, she muttered to herself as she worked. Ava never saw her eat, but some of the takeout containers from the kitchen had disappeared, as had a whole carafe of cold-drip coffee that usually lasted more than a week, even when Oliver was drinking it, too. She took the coffee toddy down from the pantry and brewed some more.

Ava wondered if Lane's behavior was normal for this phase of a painting, or if she should worry, if she should try harder to get Lane to talk, to eat, to rest, to shower. Ava hadn't seen her go outside in days.

When Lane left the front room to pace the house or use the bathroom, Ava snuck in and found old undrunk coffees, milk soured, tucked behind piles of rags, cans of paint. She found a Styrofoam box with a cheeseburger, grease congealed, one bite taken out. The sofa, pushed into the corner, was covered in a mess of throw blankets. She gathered the trash and rotting food and carried it to the kitchen, trying not to look at the painting of her mother. She rode to the store for milk, bread, peanut butter.

She locked her bike and carried the bags upstairs. As soon as she stepped inside she could sense something was different. The tension was lifted, somehow. Ava walked through to the back of the house, looking for Lane. She heard the shower running in the back bathroom.

Ava listened as Lane turned off the water, dressed, ran the hair dryer. When she came into the kitchen she appeared tired but present. She seemed to see Ava and not the things inside her head.

"Hi," Ava said. "Do you want a sandwich? I got peanut butter."

"No thanks," Lane said. "Let's go get something. Let's go up to Patois, come on."

"Go out to eat?" Ava said.

"Yeah, why not."

Lane picked up her purse, and Ava followed her out and down the steps. It had been weeks since Ava had been in a car. She settled into the passenger seat and buckled her seat belt. The click, the sight of her grandmother's hand on the steering wheel, the suffocating heat, the being taken somewhere, being close to another person after the days of brittle loneliness. Ava inhaled the hot car air, and the rush of loss overwhelmed her. She had noticed that this feeling could come over her at the unlikeliest moments, any tiny thing could bring Louise in so close it choked her. The click of a seat belt. The countless times she had been driven to school, to karate and dance, to slumber parties and the Hy-Vee to pick up something for dinner. She could not push the flood of grief aside.

Lane pulled out of the driveway and drove, expertly straddling potholes. Ava trembled, could not speak. The tears came without sounds. The blurry blocks rushed by and Lane parked near the restaurant, got out, waited. The child was always quiet, it wasn't remarkable. But Ava did not get out of the car, and Lane turned around to see this Louise-ish girl shaking, weeping, her face red and stricken. Now what. Lane went back, opened Ava's door.

"What is it?" Lane said.

Ava found that she could speak, though her voice was too loud, uncontrollable. "I miss my mom," she said. It was almost a shout, descended into sobs.

"But she's here," Lane said, blinking. A moment of honest confusion. She was looking, right now, at the lovely face of this young, too-tall Louise, who was shaking like some engine about to break apart.

"What?" said Ava.

"She's in you, she's part of you. I can't explain it. Come on, hon. Get out of the car."

Ava did as she was told and stood, weeping, on the sidewalk of Laurel Street.

"It's a nice day," Lane said, shutting the car door.

She didn't mean the weather, exactly. Not the light. Ruthless August, oppressive heat trapped by cloud cover, a threat of rain and a graying out of everything, no shadows, no contrast, only wet gray heat. She meant it was nice to be in the old neighborhood with the girl, like the feeling of realizing time didn't matter. No, that wasn't quite it. It had to do with gradations, with the past, maybe. With being almost but not quite finished with the painting. Just a feeling, too hard to explain. Lane dug in her purse for a tissue and handed it to Ava, who blew her nose.

"Let's walk a little," Lane said. "We're not far from the parrots."

Ava regarded her without comprehension, but Lane took her hand and squeezed it, and held it, and they walked. Ava had never seen Lane outside of the house before. She looked different. Younger, more a part of the city. She had an ease about her that was not present at home. It distracted Ava from her grief.

"Shit, I thought it was this block," Lane said. "Where are we?" She squinted at the street sign.

Worry crept into Ava again, the constant uncertainty she underwent around Lane—what was she ever talking about, and was the confusion Ava's or Lane's? Ava hardly ever knew, and either way there was not much she could do about it. She kept hold of Lane's hand and followed her around the corner, down another street.

"Here we are," Lane said. "The parrots."

They stood before a shotgun duplex with a shared front porch. One half of the porch was taken up entirely by a large cage. Ava saw the metal wires were bolted to the porch floor and ceiling. The people who lived here must have used the back door to get in and out—the cage had no openings that Ava could see. Parrots of many colors and sizes hopped and fluttered inside. They stood on various perches, picked at some tattered plants.

Lane said, "Hello, birdies," and a few of the parrots said "Hello, Hello." And "Pretty bird, you're a pretty bird." One of them made a sound like a truck backing up.

"They've been here since forever," Lane said to Ava. "I used to bring Louise to see them, when she was still in a stroller."

Ava stared at Lane, startled. She never mentioned Louise.

"The same birds?" Ava said.

"Could be. Parrots can live for decades. There's more of them now than there used to be. These little red ones hopping around, they didn't used to have those. But they've always had a bunch."

"They're really cool," Ava said. "Thanks for showing them to me."

"The old man who kept them died a few years ago. Now it's his daughter living here."

Ava tried to comprehend such a life. What would it be like to inherit birds, and a house. To stay in the place where they had always been. It sounded nice.

"What was she like?" Ava said. "My mom."

"She was always very serious. Responsible. A lot like you. I'm pretty sure I drove her nuts. She would have preferred a different kind of mom. I wasn't cut out for it, really."

Ava didn't know what to say to this. The neighbor's half of the porch had a hanging fern, wicker furniture, an outdoor rug straight out of a catalog. It was a funny contrast. What kind of person would decorate their porch this conventionally but live next to parrots. The idea appealed to her. Maybe the parrot people needed regular people around, and the regular people needed the parrot people.

"We should go to the restaurant," Ava said, thinking of how little Lane had eaten or slept over the last few days.

"Okay," Lane said, letting go of Ava's hand.

They passed the hardware store and saw a man come out with a small paper bag in his hand.

"There you are, darlin'," he said. "Man, it's been too long!"

Ava studied Lane, who was smiling at the man. "Ronzo, baby," Lane said. "How you been?"

He stepped in and kissed Lane on the lips. "Better now," he said. "Why you keeping yourself away from me? Working hard?"

"Working hard." Lane nodded. "How about you, that album out yet?"

"Next month. We'll have a party for it."

"Congrats, that's great."

"Glad you said that," he said. "Cause it's at your house."

Lane laughed. "Guess I'll be there, then."

"You better. You can come, too," he said to Ava. "Everyone's invited."

"This is my granddaughter," Lane said.

"I'm Ava," Ava said.

He took her hand as though to shake, then leaned down and kissed it. "Charmed," he said.

Ava giggled. "Nice to meet you," she said.

"Well, I'll let you ladies get to it. Man, what a treat to see you. I thought I was just out buying nails." He held up his paper sack.

"See you, hon," Lane said.

"Who was that guy?" Ava asked Lane.

"Oh, Ronzo. He lives in the neighborhood."

"He's your friend?"

"Sure, we were in school together."

"He was joking, right? Is he really having a party at your house?"

"Of course not."

At Patois they got a table in the window. Lane was silent through most of the meal, listlessly drinking chardonnay. At least she ate, Ava noted—a cup of gumbo and part of a sandwich. As Lane was paying the check, a woman, younger than Lane, came up to their table—she was tall, wearing high-waisted trousers and velvet boots with a cut-out toe. You'd have to look at a lot of magazines to dress like that, Ava thought.

"Lanie," the woman said. "I don't believe it!"

Lane's face brightened. She actually stood up out of her chair to give the woman a hug.

"Delia, you look gorgeous," Lane said. "How've you been?"

Ava had never heard Lane's voice sound this way, like she was smiling. She *was* smiling. She was asking this woman about her pottery studio and the woman was saying something about the exhibition space and the glazes. Lane thumbed through photos on the woman's phone.

"You were always such a talent. These are stunning. How big are they?"

"Big," the woman said, and laughed. "Check out the next one, you can see Ricardo next to it for scale."

"Oh, that's fantastic," Lane said.

"Thank you," Delia said. "That means a whole lot to me, coming from you. You should come by. I'm always there."

"I'll do that," Lane said.

The woman smiled down at Ava, seated at the table. "I'm sorry to interrupt y'all's lunch," she said. "I had to say hi."

Lane regarded Ava a beat too long. "Oh," she said. "This is—"

Lane trailed off, the smile on her face clouded with uncertainty. Ava understood.

"Hi, my name's Ava," she said to the woman. "I'm her granddaughter."

"Delia," Delia said and shook Ava's hand. "A pleasure to meet you. Are you an artist, too?"

"Um, not really," Ava said. She recognized Lane's expression—distracted, pained. "Sorry, we have to get going. Really nice to meet you."

"Lane, come by, okay? Fabulous to run into you."

Lane nodded in Delia's direction. Ava stepped toward Lane, took her hand. She waved goodbye to the woman on their way out.

"You know everybody," Ava said to Lane.

"Now you see why I don't leave the house. Can't go two blocks without being besieged."

"They seemed nice," Ava said.

"Nice? They all want things from me." She opened the car door and sat heavily behind the wheel.

CHAPTER 34

They went home and pulled into the driveway to find Oliver sitting in the rocker on the front porch. He was holding a glass of bourbon and Coke. He'd been in the house, then. He must still have a key. Ava hadn't thought to ask for it back.

"You're not supposed to be here," she said.

"Came to check on y'all, see if you need anything. How are you? How you doing, Lanie?"

"Been a while, hasn't it," Lane said to him, and went in. Oliver followed.

"Lane, he's not supposed to be here," Ava said. "Remember?"

"Give me a break, why don't you," Oliver said. He turned to Lane. "Brought you some groceries, grass. Thought you might be running low."

"Thanks," Lane said. She sat down on the living room sofa. Ava had never seen her sit in there. She mostly walked through it to get to the painting. "Front room's a mess," Lane told Oliver. "Can you put it back together? And we're out of shampoo, I think. We're out of something."

"Sure," Oliver said. "I'll check around and see what all you need."

"I bought shampoo last week," Ava said. "We don't need anything."

"For real, Iowa. Lay off for one minute. Please."

"Lane, you fired him. Remember? He stole from you, he's not supposed—"

"God, I'm beat," Lane said.

The burst of lucidity that had propelled her out of the house earlier was gone. She wasn't listening to Ava, she was not the least bit concerned to see Oliver there. Instead, she sat back on the cushions, one arm draped over the scrolled arm of the couch, the other resting in her lap. It was so rare to see her sitting still, Ava realized. Without the frenetic energy, the pacing, consumed by whatever vision she was seeing in her head, she looked skinny and old.

"Lane, do you want to maybe go lie down?" Ava said. "You could probably use some sleep."

"Can't I sit on my own goddamn sofa?" Lane said.

Oliver took the chair next to the couch, pulled a pipe and a lighter from his pocket, and handed it to Lane. She took it, lit it, handed it back.

"I missed you, Lanie," he said.

Ava stood over them. There was nothing she could do to get Oliver out if Lane didn't want him gone.

"Let's have a drink, why don't we," Lane said. She looked like she was on the verge of sleep.

"Get her something," Oliver said to Ava.

"No way. I'm not leaving you alone with her."

Oliver sighed. "Fine," he said. "Come in the kitchen with me. I'll show you how to fix a manhattan."

They went back together and Oliver mixed three drinks. He handed one to Ava. "If you're gonna bitch at me all night, at least have a drink and be civilized about it."

Ava took a sip and spat it back in her glass.

"Oh, come on. I make a great manhattan."

"You shouldn't be here," Ava said.

"It's nice to see you, too. I mean it."

"Sure. Whatever."

"Gimme that back," he said, taking her glass. "It's too strong for you."

He poured the drink into a plastic Mardi Gras cup and added ice and Coke from the two-liter bottle on the counter. He found a spoon and stirred it, then handed it back to the girl.

"Try it now, see if it needs more Coke."

Ava sipped. "It's okay, it's better this way."

"Alright, come on."

In the living room Lane's eyes were closed.

"She hasn't been sleeping much," Ava whispered.

"She goes through those phases. She'll be alright."

"She's been working nonstop," Ava said.

"That's how she used to be a lot. It means the project's going well."

The project, Ava thought. He meant her mom, on that beach Ava had never seen. Her mom was both dead and a little girl, on the beach and in the front room. Ava had seen photos taken in that room, of Christmas presents under an enormous tree, of Louise watching television on the rabbit ear set in the corner, her hair in cheesy bows.

Ava kept the album by her bed along with the packet of photos that had finally arrived from Kaitlyn. She pored over them every night—pictures of her when she was a baby with her mom and dad, pictures of the old farm.

"You've done a good job," Oliver said, startling Ava from her reverie. "With her, I mean."

"We've been fine," Ava said.

"Yeah, I see that. You're taking care of her. Somebody like Lane, you just have to be there, not get in her way, let her do her thing. It can be tough, though. For you, I mean."

The bourbon in the drink was hitting Ava. Her limbs felt watery and loose. She'd often wondered why everyone in this town was so drunk all the time. Now she was starting to get it. It let you talk to your enemy like he was a friend. Lightness, relief. Like setting down a heavy suitcase.

Ava nodded at Lane, head tilted back, asleep. "Should we wake her and get her in bed, do you think?" she asked.

Having someone to ask was a tremendous luxury. The isolation of the last few weeks and the effort of ignoring it seeped away.

"Let's let her be," Oliver said. "Come back in the kitchen. I came here to talk to you, anyway."

"Me? Why?"

"I have something to show you."

He carried Lane's drink and his own. Ava followed.

"Sit down," he said. He took his smartphone from his pocket and tapped at the screen before handing it to Ava.

"What is this?" she said.

"It's my online banking app. This is a transfer of thirty-five hundred dollars from my account to Lane's. I did it today, you can double-check hers if you don't believe me. The money's in there."

"Thirty-five hundred dollars?"

"That's all my savings. It's the first installment. I told you I'd pay her back, and I will. It's going to take a little while, but I wanted to show you I meant it."

Ava handed him the phone.

"Ava? Don't you have anything to say?"

"It's good, I guess. It's good that you're paying her back. But why? You said she wouldn't care, she wouldn't notice. She doesn't even remember it. What are you trying to do?"

"She doesn't care. It's not for her. It's for you. So you can trust me again."

"What do you care if I trust you?"

"Because you need me."

"Not really," Ava said.

"Look, Ava. You've been doing a great job. I mean it. I'm impressed. This shit ain't easy."

"We're fine without you."

"Yeah? And what happens next? School's starting soon. You need to go to school. I'm guessing you were like a straight-A student, weren't you?"

Ava shrugged.

"So you're gonna what? Drop out, stay home, and take care of Lane? Even I went to fucking high school, Ava. Would your mother want that for you? You need help. You can't even enroll in school without an adult to help you. Try getting Lane to do that shit."

"I can manage," Ava said, but he was right. The summer was ending soon. School would start and she couldn't care for Lane alone.

"Now, maybe. How about when she gets worse?"

"We'll figure it out."

"Right. Good luck with that." At least she was listening, wasn't trying to kick him out. "Hey," he said. "Let's do something. Let's play cards."

"Why?"

"Why not? It's fun. You don't have to be suspicious of everything I say. Do you know gin?"

"No," she said.

"I'll teach you. There's cards in that long drawer in the pantry."

"I know where they are," she said.

"Course you do."

She found a couple of ancient decks and they went through them, counting, to make sure they were complete. They played a practice game, showing their cards, then another one to teach her how to knock. The first two real hands, he let her win, let her tally the score. She made neat columns, tidy arithmetic. He finished his cocktail and started on Lane's. Ava was still sipping her whiskey and Coke. She won the third hand on her own and Oliver started to concentrate. The girl was smart, a fast learner.

"So, hey. There's something else I need to discuss with you. While Lane's asleep."

"What?" Ava said.

"I've put this off too long already, but I'm going to take her to see a doctor."

Fear hit Ava in the stomach. "Why?"

"Well. I should've done it already. Maybe they can figure out what's wrong with her. Maybe there's something they can do. At least they could tell us what to expect."

"She won't go."

"She has to. I think it's past the point of letting her decide."

Ava took this in, nodded. "At least let her finish the painting first," she said.

"Yeah, I will. It's almost done. It's so fucking good. She's amazing."

"I know," Ava said. "Anyways, gin."

She laid her cards down, four jacks and two runs. She'd caught him out, he'd been waiting on the jack of diamonds.

"Shit," he said. "You got me. Forty-three."

He watched her add up the points with grim deliberation. He could see the strange whiteness of her skin in the part of her hair.

"See what I mean?" he said. "You can't deal with this on your own. Nobody can, it's too hard."

"Can I ask you something?" she said. "Why'd you take all that money? How could you steal from her?"

"Damn, girl. Let's have a nice time for a minute, okay?"

"The thing I don't get is, you seem like you actually do care about her. How can you do it? Unless you're faking the whole thing?"

"I do care. I love Lane. I've never met anybody like her. She's . . ." He paused, drank, trying to figure out how to say it. "She's a force. She's like a storm, like a tide, maybe. You can't tell her anything, but just being around her . . . it's really something."

"Then how could you do it?" She seemed genuinely curious.

"What," he said. "You never hurt somebody you loved? You never acted like an asshole?"

"No," Ava said. "Not on purpose."

"God, you can really be sanctimonious sometimes, farm girl." He said it softly, kindly. "You know she doesn't care. I would never take something from her that she needed."

"I know, but—"

"But what? It's not right? *She* doesn't care. Maybe you should try not caring, too. You're wearing yourself out with it. Think how much easier things would be if you quit worrying about this shit."

"You have a messed-up way of thinking," she said. Her prim posture had a wobble to it. Her drink was nearly gone.

"I'm not a bad person," Oliver said. "I realize you think I am, but I'm not."

"I don't think you're bad. That's why I don't understand it. You could've just not done it and everything would be better."

"You're right, you're right. I'm trying to fix it, though, I swear. Try to trust me. Think you can do that?"

"I don't know. What's gonna happen to us?" Ava said.

"Shit. Why you asking me? I don't even work here anymore."

She gave him a look of disdain.

"Hey, there you go, roll your eyes at me. You're finally starting to act like a normal teenager."

Before she could answer, Lane appeared in the doorway. She came in, picked up the pipe, and lit it.

"What's going on here?" she said.

"We're playing gin. Li'l Farm Girl is killing me."

"I'll take one of those," Lane said, pointing at Oliver's cocktail. "Guess I took a nap. I hate waking up when it's dark outside." She hit the pipe and set it on the counter. "What time is it, anyway?"

"Nine thirty," Ava said.

"Why, you gotta be somewhere?" Oliver said.

"I s'pose not," Lane said.

Oliver mixed her drink, fishing a maraschino cherry from a jar in the fridge. Ava noted the red drips he left on the counter and imagined them tomorrow, dried and sticky, envisioned wiping them away. Reordering the house in his wake. He handed Lane the drink.

"Hey," Ava said. "What about me?" She held her empty cup out to Oliver. He poured in Coke over ice, skipping the bourbon this time. Maybe she could trust him after all. Oliver was right, it would make things a whole lot easier.

CHAPTER 35

The second letter rested on a pile of mail in Artie's office. He'd been awaiting it ever since the first one. He had wondered what he would do when it came, and he watched himself now, still curious. He closed the outer door before slitting the envelope open. He read it through three times, his eyes returning to the number listed there. The shape of it, the space it took up on the page had a magnetized intensity that drew him. It centered his attention. He breathed in, exhaled. It was as though his breath took the shape of the number, he could feel the number expanding his lungs.

He scanned the office. The crowd of people had thinned out, the volunteer teams dispatched to their various locations for the day. Albertine was at her desk, typing and talking on the phone. Marley was pacing, fielding calls from her volunteers. Artie thought about his agenda. He had meetings set up, interviews, a lunch with the Orleans Parish school board superintendent, and he planned to do some personal door-to-door visits in Broadmoor and Mid-City in the afternoon. Well, there was a new priority, now.

He opened his office door, leaned out. Kirk, Albertine's

assistant, was hovering over a box of doughnuts by the coffee station.

"Hey, Kirk, got a second?" he said.

"Yes, sir!" Kirk said, startled and blushing. He hurried over, dusting sugar from the front of his shirt.

"I need to rearrange my schedule, push back my appointments to tomorrow. Or later in the week. Check with Albertine, she has the details."

"Sure thing."

"And please give the superintendent my apologies. I'm going out, y'all can reach me on my cell."

Kirk was nodding vigorously, anxious to please.

"Thanks for all your effort," Artie said. "You're doing a great job." He smiled the smile that made everyone happy.

"Thank you, sir. I mean, you're welcome. I mean, thanks."

"Keep it up," Artie said, turning away, dismissing him. He hoped to escape the office before interacting with anyone else. He gathered his things and hurried past Marley, Albertine, and Kirk, who was now on the phone, too, canceling appointments. The bustle of the headquarters was impeding Artie's thought process. He was good under pressure, he reminded himself. He just needed to think.

He got in his car, put it in gear, and headed toward the lake. He drove past the Southern Yacht Club to the Point and parked. This was where the Lakeview and Metairie teens came at night to party, to get drunk and make out while waves crashed around their cars. He'd been down here himself as a kid, before he'd gone east. Now, midmorning, it was abandoned. He took the letter out of his pocket and examined it. His hands shook. He resisted the impulse to tear up the page, to throw it in the water.

This new letter was asking for $150,000, and who was to say it wouldn't escalate? It wasn't sustainable. For the first time, the word *ruin* arose in Artie's mind. As in, *This could ruin me.* The single feasible option was to figure out who this person was, and put an end to it.

That sensation again, of the decades shrinking down to a pinprick. The bleeding man in Artie's arms, like he'd always been there, like he'd never gone away. The man's head in Artie's lap, blood glistening in headlights. How the weight of the man changed, became heavier, how the ragged breath had ceased and Artie understood the man had died. That weight bored a hole in Artie that he felt himself falling into. Jesus, he was crying now. He looked around to check that he was still alone.

He forced himself past that memory, but what happened next was a blank. He must have found a pay phone, he must have paged his father, because his father had taken care of it. Had known what to do.

He tried to think. It was like straining to recall the plot of a movie he'd once seen. The sense of unreality was strong. The details got blotted out by the man's face, blood slick on Artie's arms and legs, later dried and itchy, crusting his clothes. He'd been taken somewhere after. He couldn't recall how he got there. He remembered a useless image, he was standing in a shower, blood diluted, running over white and black hexagonal tiles, flower patterns in the floor. If only his father were alive . . . Artie cut off the thought. It wasn't the time for pointless grieving.

He got out, walked around the car, stretching his legs, putting himself back in the present. He was not that boy. He was thirty-four years old, talented, handsome, strong. His family loved him, his city loved him. This letter was a problem, and Artie excelled at fixing problems. He could deal with this. He had to, and then he would win. He would rise farther than his father. He had everything he would need. Stamina, vision, the love of the people. He let the faint hot breeze coming off the lake travel over him.

Where was that house? He shook out his arms, ridding them of the weight of the dying man. He paced in front of the car, watched the lake lap against the concrete barrier.

He closed his eyes. He was fourteen, his hair wet after the shower. He was wearing borrowed clothes, paint-splattered shorts, a fun run T-shirt, no shoes. He sat at a kitchen table with a woman, his father's lover. Paint was under her nails and etched into the calluses of her hands. The clothes he wore belonged to her. He'd never learned her name, of this he was certain. Later, his father was there and they had gone down the steps. A raised house, then. The front seat of his father's car smelled of a harsh chemical cleaning agent—of course, he must have ridden in it with his bloodied clothes, and his father would have cleaned it. Through his shock, he remembered having recognized the neighborhood. Half a block from where his friend Jacob used to live, until seventh grade, when Jacob's family had moved to Shreveport. He had ridden his scooter past the woman's house with Jacob hundreds of times, on their way to get sno-balls.

He surveyed the lake. A pickup truck came down the Breakwater road and parked a little ways from him. He watched the man get out and retrieve a fishing pole, a camp chair, and a tackle box from the truck bed. Artie did not want to be recognized, not when he was agitated like this. He got back in the car, checked his phone. A few text messages from the office, nothing urgent. He would sit here in the driver's seat and run the A/C until his sweat dried, and then he would go somewhere and buy himself some lunch. This afternoon he would do as he planned, knock on doors, introduce himself to voters. His trunk was stuffed with flyers, buttons, business cards, shirts, each emblazoned with his image. He had everything he needed. He would keep campaigning, keep thinking, until he figured out what to do.

The rest of the day was restorative. His sense of himself gradually returned, so by the time he drove home at the end of the day and hugged his girls and kissed Marisol, who was making grilled redfish and corn on the cob with a tomato salad for dinner, he was as he'd been that morning, before he'd opened the envelope. He ate with his family, put the kids to bed, made a few follow-up calls to potential campaign donors, then sat down with his wife. She poured him a glass of wine. They chatted about their day—Mari told a funny story about her yoga class, said she'd spent forever in Target buying the girls new swimsuits. Artie was fine, he was sure he was acting the way he always did, and Marisol didn't notice anything amiss. He went to bed at ten, had no trouble drifting to sleep.

In the middle of the night he opened his eyes. His heart going like he was in the middle of a run. The white noise machine in their bedroom whispered steadily. By his side Marisol slept. He could not remember his dream, only a sense of deep disturbance. He got out of bed, checked on the kids. Both asleep. In the kitchen he poured a whiskey from the engraved crystal decanter on the sideboard. It had been a wedding gift. They had so many nice things. His suit coat was hanging on the back of a chair. He reached in the inside pocket and retrieved the letter.

Noiselessly he opened the door to the backyard and went out. He sat on the bench and stared into the faces of ghostly ginger flowers, their strange finger shapes throwing long shadows in the streetlight. It was three, four in the morning. He sipped his drink. Marisol had left the lighter that she'd used to start the coals for dinner outside. He picked it up, flicked it, and touched the tidy flame to the paper. He dropped it on the grill and watched it burn. His heart was beating normally now.

Artie downed the last of the whiskey in his glass. Before he went to bed he retrieved the lockbox from the top shelf in their attached garage and opened it with his key. He took out the pistol, loaded it, and put it in the glove box of his car. He would canvass Uptown tomorrow, wind his way toward the river from St. Charles, starting around State or Nashville, find the house in daylight. Form a plan.

He slept solidly until his alarm woke him. He laced his running shoes, refreshed and confident. Another day. This city was his. He was going to win the election. One bad night decades ago was not going to get in the way.

CHAPTER 36

Lane worked. There was nothing but the painting, nothing but Louise. The girl brought coffee, but Lane ended up sticking her brushes in the cup by accident, and, irritated, set it on the floor outside the room. She was lucky to have the big live oak outside, the way its leaves diffused the light. Sharp-edged leaf shadows trembled over the wall where Louise stood by the bay, and Lane traced their gestures in the water and the sand and the folds of her daughter's sundress. The painting belonged in this room, in this house, in this light.

She had not painted with this kind of urgency since she was a much younger woman. She knew she was making something good. Really good. She lost herself in it, she didn't know where it came from, yet she brought all her skills to bear. Her trapezius muscles ached, she was using her entire arm, the brush saturated with paint, wetter and longer gestures than she usually made. It felt right. This one last time, she thought. This could be the last one I finish, the last one that's good.

Lane woke from a nap, found herself lying on the front room sofa, surrounded by floor lamps and tables and chairs pushed into the corner. The sky was blooming into shades of pink and purple, softening over the ceiling. Outside, car doors closed, people were coming home from work. She was thirsty. She got up, stretching her sore muscles, avoiding the mural. It would not do, to look at it too soon. She opened the door and kicked over a cup of coffee someone had set on the floor. She swore, left it there, soaking into the rug.

In the kitchen she drank two glasses of water. The house was too still, and sounds from the neighborhood drew her outside. She stepped over some kind of sticky mess, coffee or paint or both, and opened the front door. She walked out, down the steps, into late summer twilight: smoke from grills, lawn mowers, and leaf blowers. So much motion and noise. She ambled along the buckled sidewalk, the route she used to take Louise's little dog. Couldn't think of the name of that one, though with no effort she saw its little white face and the fur growing over its dirty paws.

She walked until the street dead-ended into Henry Clay. She skirted the walls of the hospital grounds that took up three city blocks. Tiny ferns growing out of the brick here and there. They would disintegrate the mortar eventually if no one pulled them out. Everything around her inclined toward dissolution, solid walls slumped in the swamp air. At the park she ignored the joggers on the trail, all those people and their striving. She cut across the grass to the lagoon. Ducks fought at the bank for bits of bread. She picked her way over the tree roots and squinted across at Bird Island. Sometimes you could see egrets in their nests, but maybe it was the wrong season. Anyway, now the light was too dim.

The sky reflected on the water interested her. It kept shifting. She used to bring Lulu down here with old heels of bread to feed the ducks, when she was hardly bigger than they were. Louise had never been afraid of them. Even as a three-year-old she'd let them eat out of her hand. What a creature she was, little Louise. How enormous, this loss. Darkness crept around the tree roots, caught and clung to the negative space between trunks. Funny how the night always started in pockets, in corners, and spread out from there.

Maybe the painting was finished. She thought it might be.

It was pleasant to be outside in the dusk. Cooler, especially near the water. She could bring a sketchbook out here, even an easel and canvas, try some plein air painting. Something different. The thing about these pockets of darkness, they telegraphed the end: shadows spread over every open space, every trail and puddle and bird, the gardens and the roofs, they spread like a bruise over every corner of her mind. It might be possible to capture it before it was too late. If she worked fast, if she painted the dark instead of the light. She could come tomorrow, carry her supplies.

She rose, her joints creaking, and made her way home. There had to be a pile of canvases somewhere, an old painting she could gesso over. She could get a couple of coats on it tonight and another in the morning. Or she could run up to the store and buy one already stretched and prepped. They were expensive but that's what money was for. She could tell Oliver to go by there first thing.

The sky through the trees on her block still glowed a faint purple. She crossed her yard, automatically stepping over the roots of the oak as she'd done since she was a child. When she entered the house she was alarmed to find it empty. Where was everybody? Where was her papa, he ought to be back by now. Maybe he was in Baton Rouge on a business trip, or he'd been called away after dinner, some emergency at the office. She peered out the window, to see if his car was in the driveway. There was a car there, and beyond it, standing on the sidewalk where there had been no one a moment ago, was the solid, un-mistakable form of Bert, staring up at the windows.

Heat flooded her at the sight of him. He'd been gone for so long and now he was back, here to see her. The gift of him, right here—it nearly knocked her over. Why didn't he come inside? He turned to look across the street, up and down the block, and then back to her house. Strange, he usually approached from the alley, took precautions, but now he stood out front where any-body could see. Something must have happened. Some piece of bad news. In a flutter of alarm she wondered where Louise was, did something happen to Louise?

"Lane," Louise said, as though Lane had conjured her up with her thoughts.

"Good, you're here."

"Why are you standing in the dark?"

"It just got dark," Lane said.

"No, it's almost ten o'clock."

Lane sighed, already sick of her daughter and this tendency she had, to always be right. Still, Lane was surprised at the hour, she'd lost track of the time. The girl turned on the lights, asked if she was hungry.

Lane was glad the lights were on, that way Bert would see she was home, that Louise was here. She hoped he would come back later. Why hadn't he called? Had he called?

"Lane," she said. "Come eat something, okay? You haven't eaten since breakfast."

Lane forced herself to turn away from the window. He was still out there, but he had stepped into the shadows and she saw only her reflection. She took in the room. It was in disarray, nothing where it should be.

"Did someone break in?" Lane said. "Have we been robbed?"

"What?"

"Can't you see? The sofa is pushed to the wall, look at the tables, everything's a mess."

"Lane, it's okay, you did it. For the painting."

She pointed to the wall and Lane saw it then. Louise in a painting where a painting was not supposed to be. It was half-miraculous, strange shapes played out over the planes, the forms utterly tangible. Like you could step into it, take the crawfish from her hand and brush the sand off her dress and take her in your lap and hear her little serious voice. Like you could step past her and keep going, enter the water and sink to your knees, let it lap warm around your shoulders. Like that was real and this room was the illusion, unspeckled as it was with sand and beachlight. She squinted at the girl and saw she was not Louise at all, Louise was only in the painting.

"Who are you?" Lane said, suddenly anxious.

"It's me, Ava. Louise's girl." She smiled. "It's beautiful." She was looking at the painting. "Where is it? Is the beach a real place, or did you make it up?"

"It's in Alabama," Lane said. "Perdido Bay. We always went there. Don't you know it?"

The girl shook her head.

Louise's girl. Loss cascaded around Lane. Wasn't everyone here, just a moment ago? Where was her daughter, where was Bert, where was Oliver? Why had she trapped her daughter in this painting where she could not be got at?

"It's too much," she said.

"I know," Ava said, her voice tender. "You need to eat. Come on."

The girl came and took her by the arm, led her back through the house. At the table this stranger with the long limbs and the same straight hair as Louise set a plate before her—chicken salad, a bunch of grapes, some kind of pointy crunchy things, whatever they were called. The stranger poured a glass of Coke from a two-liter bottle on the counter, handed Lane the drink and a paper towel folded in quarters. Lane chewed the food while the girl watched. It was exhausting, this life. How did anyone manage it?

"Put a little bourbon in that, why don't you?" she said to the girl.

"Two more bites, then I will."

Lane didn't have the energy to argue. She was hungry, she supposed, though the food tasted like nothing. The pale dull colors of it. She shoved another bite into her mouth, chewed, swallowed. What was going on with time today? she wondered. Some moments took forever and others seemed to have been skipped entirely. But here, here was a real drink the girl handed her, finally. Plenty strong. Girl didn't know how to fix a proper drink, but that was alright. The whiskey hit her and that explained the strangeness, she was a little drunk, that was all.

She hoped Bert would come back after the girl was in bed. It had been too long since she had seen him. Some days, the aloneness and the effort of her life cut at her and she began to regret everything. Letting him marry someone else. Why hadn't she kept him for herself? Maybe it wouldn't have been a disaster, maybe they could have been happy. The girl was back, touching her shoulder.

"Why don't you go to bed, Lane. You're falling asleep at the table."

"No, I'm not," she said.

But she heaved herself up, went down the hall, brushed her teeth, the whole routine. She found her pipe, already loaded, sitting on the dresser in her bedroom. She went out to the balcony to smoke. The house was dark, the dishes drying in the rack, no sign of the girl. Her legs stretched out, feet propped on the railing. The bowl went out and after some time she lit it again. How much of her existence had she spent waiting?

Finally he appeared. Pushed the back gate open and crept out from the shadow of the neighbors' shed. She watched him; she could tell he hadn't seen her yet. His movements were strange, hesitant. He nearly stumbled over the uneven pavers, caught himself. Maybe he was drunk. She didn't care, she wanted his arms around her, she wanted to hear his voice, to tell him her new idea for a painting. He was even with the house now, right below her. She expected to hear him on the steps but he didn't even glance up, instead he opened the door to the basement. It scraped the cement pad down there—the door must be sagging, something new she'd have to fix.

But why was he going down there? She held still, listening. She couldn't hear him anymore, so she went in. The floor would creak under her, above his head, telling him she was here, in the kitchen, waiting in the dark. He opened the door from the basement to the hall, creeping, cautious. From the end of the long hallway, she said, "Hey, I'm back here."

He jumped at the sound of her voice, and then came toward her. Something off about the way he carried himself.

"What's going on?" she said, whispering, so as not to rouse the sleeping girl. They had always been quiet together in the night.

"You tell me," he said, and the voice was wrong; everything was wrong.

She flipped the light switch and flooded the kitchen in a yellow glow. He stood in front of her. It wasn't Bert. It was the son, whose face was everywhere these days.

Lane recoiled. He had Bertrand's build but his mother's face. The warmth, the desire, turned to poison in her stomach.

"It's you," he said. "I remember you."

"What are you doing in my house?" Lane said.

"Did you really think I wouldn't find you?" he said.

Lane shrugged. It was one of those situations that wasn't adding up. She didn't think he was supposed to be here, but maybe she'd forgotten some arrangement? She tried to think.

"We need to talk," he said. "Face-to-face. I'm not doing that movie bullshit like before, leave the bag behind a Dumpster. I have it, I'll hand it over, but this is the last time."

The last time? They'd done this before, then. But why? His presence in her kitchen was an abomination, unclean.

"You shouldn't be here," she said. "I never wanted this."

The man laughed, bitter, incredulous. "You should have thought of that before," he said.

Lane went to the phone on the wall, to call Bert, get him over here, stop whatever this was from happening.

"Your father . . ." she said, but the phone wasn't there, a small painting of the sea hung where it used to be.

"What about my father?" He sounded angry now, his voice tinged with disgust. "You had an affair, right? I figured that out years ago. I'm not interested in talking about my father with you. Sit down. I'll tell you how this is going to go."

Lane sat at the table. The man, Artie, was holding one of those mailer envelopes with the bubble wrap inside, stuffed with something bulky. He set it on the table between them, pushed it toward her.

"Here's the one fifty."

The one-fifty? The words were meaningless to Lane. Nevertheless she put her hand on the envelope. It felt solid, like paperback books.

"It's all there, feel free to count it."

She regarded the envelope, trying to piece the situation together. She was waiting for her mind to catch up, for things to click into place. But then, as she watched him, he reached into his pocket and pulled from it a dull black pistol. It seemed to eat the light in the room, take the air from her lungs.

"I don't want to hurt you," he said, "but I will. Tell me who else knows."

Bert would kill him for threatening her. This little shit.

"Your father . . ." Lane said.

"Shut up about my father. Just tell me who you told. Did you tell anybody else?"

"He doesn't know you're here."

"Who doesn't? Who did you talk to?"

Lane didn't answer, she was distracted by an image. Bert's name etched in the stone of a tomb. She had pressed her hand against it, felt the heat. None of this should be happening.

Bert was gone. Dead. The man stared at her, she couldn't think of his name now, but she hated seeing the shape of Bert's shoulders, here in this stranger. It was a cruelty, it pierced her. The clock on the wall read one in the morning, the dishrag wrung out and hung over the faucet, someone else had done that, not her. Nothing in the kitchen helped her understand.

"Answer me," he said, jerking the gun in her direction.

She almost laughed. "Go ahead. You've taken everything from me already."

"Lady," he said. "What the hell are you talking about?"

"Louise saw everything. I had to tell her. She was good, do you understand? She wasn't like us. She knew the difference between right and wrong. It's your fault she left."

"You told her? What did she see?"

"What do you think? You, bloody, stumbling through the house. She saw us together, saw me helping you. It doesn't matter anymore. She's gone. Wouldn't talk to me after that."

"Yes, it fucking matters," he said. "Where is she?"

All the loss Lane had withstood came forth into her body. She shook with fury.

"You have no right to know anything about her. You're the reason she left. Now she's dead. Like your father. She never came back. All because of you."

"It's not my fault," he said. "I was a kid."

"Shut up. I kept your secret for Bert. But now—you took her from me and now you come back here? You threaten me? Get out of my house, or I'll tell everyone what you did."

He looked at her, astonished, then down at the gun in his hand. It was like she'd forgotten it was there. He raised it and pointed it at her face. Then she saw it. Then she understood. She ran into the hallway, toward the front of the house. He caught up easily, grabbed her arm. It hurt where he held her. It would bruise, her skin was so thin these days.

"Let go," she said.

Her legs were rubbery, her skin cold. Her knees buckled, but he held her upright. She cried out. He lost his balance and brushed the wall, knocking her uncle's old watercolors askew. They were abreast of the basement door.

Lane struggled, yelled. He held her from behind, his arm around her throat, trying to keep her still, make her shut up. The dim basement steps spilled below her, it reminded her of something, the darkness. She kicked at him and made contact with something, his knee, his leg. She heard him curse, then the shot drowned out sound. A soft streetlight glow came up from the basement window, and pockets of dark covered everything.

CHAPTER 37

Ava woke. She heard voices from the back of the house, Lane talking to someone, a man. At first, sleepy and disoriented, she thought it was Oliver. But the man didn't sound like Oliver. A break-in, like Lane was always afraid of. Ava went for her phone first, but it wasn't there. She'd left it in the living room, connected to a power cord. A thump came from the hallway, and the sound of Lane arguing with the man. She sounded scared, though Ava couldn't discern the words.

Ava knelt in the bed and reached in the pocket of the pioneer girl costume for the pistol, drew it out, opened the chamber. The bullets were still there, too, where she'd put them months ago. She loaded the gun, unsure what to do next. Stay put? Hide? Go for the phone? But when she heard Lane cry out she reacted, already holding the gun steady, cocked, moving toward the sound of her grandmother's voice. She stepped into the dining room and saw, in the hall, a man holding Lane. Before Ava could do a thing, he shot Lane and pushed her down the basement steps.

Ava shrieked. The man turned, startled, faced her.

"It was an accident," he said. He held his hands out to her, his right hand still holding the gun. He gawked at it, bewildered.

"Lane," Ava said.

The man registered the gun in Ava's hand and took a step closer. She tightened her grip, steadied her aim.

"No," the man said, coming toward her now. "She should never have—why was she—?"

"Is Lane okay?" She asked the question, even though she'd seen.

"I didn't mean to," he said. His hands were out, he was reaching for Ava. Getting too close.

Ava closed her eyes, saw her grandmother in his arms before him and then in a blink just gone, disappeared through the basement door. The thump of her body down the steps and then the silence.

She fired once, twice. Her father's training kicked in, she'd done it right, exhaled and held her arm steady, aimed for the broadest target, the center of his chest. The man went down. Ava held still, watching him. He wasn't moving or making a sound but she kept the gun on him. She didn't know how long she stood there. She took a breath in, she had forgotten to inhale. She had to check on Lane.

Ava descended the basement steps, where she could see her grandmother crumpled below. She sank to the bottom step and gathered Lane into her arms. She knew Lane was dead but she held her and held her, just the same. No sound came from upstairs. Ava would have to go back up, find the phone and call someone, Oliver or the police. A remote part of her brain mapped it out: she would lay Lane's head on the basement floor, climb the steps, go to the living room, pick up the phone and call Oliver's number, and hope he picked up. She would keep calling him until he did. She would have to think about the man upstairs, she would have to walk past him, think about what she had done to him, explain it to someone else.

She understood she would need to do these things, but that was in the future. Now she held her grandmother, she smoothed Lane's hair away from her face. Gravity held them to the basement floor. Ava's arms assumed a sole purpose: to hold Lane. Hold her and not let her go.

CHAPTER 38

Oliver had just gotten to sleep when the phone rang. It took him a minute to piece together what Ava was telling him, that he needed to come over, it had to be now. He was really past too drunk to drive, but the kid wouldn't call him this late unless it was a real emergency. Something with Lane, he wouldn't let himself think about what. Carefully he maneuvered the car through the streets, windows down, hoping the humid breeze would refresh him. At Lane's he let himself in. The house was dark. Something was different in the air. Unsettled.

"Lanie," he called out, softly because it was late, nearly three in the morning. "Ava? Lane?"

No one answered but he heard a noise, a shuffling. He turned on the light. "Lane," he called, louder. The sound had come from the back, maybe the basement. He walked toward the hall and saw the figure on the floor, a man's crumpled form, a pool of dark blood.

"Christ," Oliver said. "Fuck. Ava! Lane!" he was yelling now.

He turned away from the corpse, glanced back at it. Oliver couldn't see the face, but the man was clearly dead. The sound came again, a whimper. The basement door stood open. Definitely coming from below. Oliver pulled the string for the basement light and descended the steps. Ava and Lane were down here, hiding. There was an intruder and he somehow had been shot, and Ava and Lane were safe.

"Lane," Oliver said, "what the fuck happened?" He could see them huddled together on the floor at the bottom of the steps, but they didn't answer him.

"Come on, let's get y'all upstairs," Oliver said. He leaned down, put his hand on Ava's back. She jumped, made a frightened sound, the same cry he'd heard from upstairs.

"Whoa, whoa, it's just me. It's Oliver. It's okay. Come on, get up. You, too, Lanie. It's safe now. You're safe."

The bare bulb over the stairs was insufficient. Oliver moved around the heap of them, crouched down in order to see. Lane was lying on the floor, her head in Ava's lap, and the girl wouldn't look up. His vision was adjusting to the dark. He could see Lane better now, her eyes were closed. He touched her arm, and it lay there inert.

"She's passed out," he said. "We'll take her to the ER. We can go around the side, straight out to the car. We don't have to go upstairs. What happened, Ava?"

She shook her head.

"Okay, I'll carry her. Are you hurt? Can you walk?"

She turned her face toward him, but it was like she wasn't seeing him.

"It's okay," he said.

He gathered Lane into his own lap. He felt the blood, realized she wasn't breathing. He checked her pulse, couldn't find it. She wasn't unconscious. Lane was dead.

The girl was visibly shaking, now that she was no longer holding her grandmother. A pistol lay in her lap. He placed Lane's head down gently and reached over to take the gun. Jesus fuck, he said. Fucking Christ. He slipped it in his waistband and got to his feet. He pulled Ava up and gathered her in his arms, found that she was able to stand, that she would let him turn her and walk her to the door. He pushed it open and they stepped into the backyard, its riot of dusty overgrown foliage edged in streetlight. He guided her through the side yard and opened the gate.

"We'll go in through the front. Can you go up the steps?"

She nodded.

"Say yes," he said. "Let me hear your voice."

"Yes."

"Good, you can talk. That's good. Come on."

They entered the house and turned into the front room with the painting. He sat her down on the couch and explained how he was going to leave her alone in there for a minute to get them both something to drink. She didn't say anything.

"Stay here," he said. "I'll be right back. It's going to be okay."

Oliver put the gun on the dining table. He went into the hallway, approached the man. His face was visible from this angle. Oliver recognized him. Fucking Art Guidry. What the hell. Oliver backed away from the man, the coagulating pool of blood. He saw Lane's pipe on the counter when he was locking the French doors and picked it up reflexively to take a hit, but then thought better of it. *Got to sober up,* he told himself. *Get your shit together. Think.*

First things first, take care of the girl. Figure out what the fuck happened, then figure out what to do.

He closed the door between the dining room and the back hall, which had always stood open, so the girl would not have to see the corpse. He made himself coffee. He found a package of Oreos and brought them to Ava along with a glass and the bourbon bottle. Sugar would help, they could both use some sugar. She sat as he'd left her, staring at the scuffed floor in front of her. Her whole body was vibrating, a high-frequency hum of panic. He poured her a shot.

"Ava," he said. "Hey, come on. Drink this, it'll make you feel better." He took her hand and put the glass of bourbon in it. "Drink the whole thing. One big sip."

She did it, coughing a little. He poured her some more. "Now this one. Then eat a cookie."

She drank the second shot and handed him the glass. He gave her a cookie and watched her chew and swallow. He sat down next to her and put his arm around her shivering shoulders. "These cookies are terrible," he said. "Who lets Oreos go stale?"

Ava shrugged her shoulders, then shivered and started to cry.

"Okay," he said. "You're in there after all."

He let her cry, relieved that her silence was over. He held her, concentrating on the moment, rubbing his hand over her bony back. His awareness drifted to Lane in the basement, Artie in the hallway, then seized up in grief and shock. He wrenched his thoughts back to the present moment. The girl. Her sobs subsided gradually.

Oliver said, "You think you can tell me what happened?"

She nodded, began, haltingly, to speak. Her voice sounded remote, high and feathery, like she was describing a dream while still half asleep. She was reciting facts but she wasn't thinking about what she was saying. When she was finished, Oliver made her eat another cookie and go over the details again. He wasn't thinking, either, not about Lane or Artie or what would happen next. His whole attention opened to Ava's words, he was memorizing everything she said. He asked questions, to make sure he had it right. *What did you hear?* he asked her. *What time was this? Where was the gun? Where were the bullets? What did you see when you came out of the hall?* She answered him, staring at a spot on the floor a few feet in front of her.

Oliver's drunkenness faded, replaced by a new state of unreality. Like he was back in Katrina time, a numbed-out, sloweddown hellscape where nothing made sense. Now he knew every detail, as though he'd been there himself: the man backlit by the dim sconce at the end of the hall. The way he'd held Lane in front of him as he faced the basement stairs. His single, seamless motion as he shot her, threw her down, and turned when he heard Ava. The weight of the gun in Ava's hand. Heavy, cold.

"Did he say anything to you?" Oliver asked.

"He said it was an accident."

"What about to Lane? Did he say anything to her? Did he say what he was doing here?"

"I heard them talking," she said. "That's what woke me up. But I couldn't hear what he said."

"Have you ever seen him before?"

"It was dark. I couldn't really see. Why? Who is he?"

"I don't know," Oliver said.

He poured her a little more whiskey. It was helping, he could tell. Her hands weren't shaking as much, and she even turned her head to look at him once or twice. She was really freaking him out when he'd first gotten her upstairs—locked inside herself, barely aware of her surroundings, but he thought she might be okay now. He'd get some real food in her, some coffee, get her out of here.

He hugged the girl close. She really was something. She was strong. She'd make it through this.

"Okay, Ava. Here's what's going to happen next. You listening?"

"Yeah," Ava said.

"First thing is, you need to take a hot shower, wash your hair, put on some clean clothes. Think you can do that?"

Ava nodded yes.

"Good. Then we'll get your stuff together."

"Why?"

"It's time to go back to Iowa," he said.

She didn't say anything, just stared at him.

"You still got minutes on your phone?"

"Yeah."

"Let me see it."

She retrieved it from the living room and handed it to Oliver, then went to shower. He examined the phone. Christ, she'd hardly used it. The girl really had no friends. Oliver called her a cab. It wasn't yet five in the morning and he had to try a couple of different companies before he found one that answered. He arranged for a car to come in forty-five minutes to the Children's Hospital entrance on Henry Clay. He assembled two peanut butter and honey sandwiches and put them in a bag with the rest of the cookies.

Ava came out with wet hair, dressed in clean clothes.

"Good girl," he said. "Now, pack. Gather up everything you brought here. Get your stuff out of the bathroom. Bring your bags up front."

"Okay," Ava said.

"Don't worry about folding anything. Just stuff it in your bags. Hurry."

Oliver went through the house, double-checking for Ava's stray belongings. In the kitchen he saw the envelope, opened it.

"Fuck," he said.

Fifteen bound stacks of hundreds, he pulled them out and fanned them. No time to think of what it meant, what he'd done. No time to feel. He pulled out two bundles and jammed them in his pocket. He put the rest back in the envelope and sealed it. He retraced his steps, taking the long way around to avoid Guidry lying there.

Ava retrieved her backpack and small suitcase and filled them with clothes, her toothbrush and comb, and the photo album with the pictures of her mother. These activities allowed her to get through the moments. Carrying herself from one moment into the next was essential, the only relevant task. She found herself standing in the living room, gazing at the closed door to the hallway. She'd never even noticed there was a door there—it had not been closed all summer. A four-paneled door, as old as the house. The peeling white paint revealed a pale green patch underneath. She wanted to point it out to Lane, to say, *The door was green, when was that, when was my mom was little?* Even though it was covered up, it was still green underneath. This house kept its past inside it.

Oliver found her standing there, staring. He took her hand, put something in it. A stack of money, she didn't know how much. The green door stood guard from behind its facade of chipping white. It hid the body of the man she had killed.

"Put this somewhere safe," he said. "Don't let anybody steal it."

He watched Ava divide up the bills and put half in each front pocket of her jeans. He handed her a thick envelope and a marker.

"Write down your address in Iowa," he said. "Put your name at the top."

She addressed the envelope.

"Your mom's friend, what's her name, Kaitlyn?"

Ava nodded.

"You trust her?"

"Yes."

"Okay, then."

The sky was getting light. Oliver handed her the envelope and the bag of sandwiches. He turned her around, guided her to the front door.

"You know the Children's Hospital by the park?"

"Yes," she said.

"Go to the main entrance on Henry Clay. There will be a cab there for you. Okay?"

"Okay."

"Tell him to take you to the post office first. The main one on Loyola, by the train station. It opens pretty early. Tell the cab to wait for you. Stay there until it opens and mail the package. Overnight it, don't worry about how much it costs. You've got enough there. You with me?"

"Yes."

"Then tell the cab to take you to the airport. Go up to a ticket counter, try American or Delta or whatever, and tell them you need to buy a ticket to Iowa City."

"There's no airport there," Ava said.

"Okay, then where do people fly to?"

"Cedar Rapids."

"Buy a ticket to Cedar Rapids. Tell them how old you are, you won't need to show ID. Once they sell you the ticket, call Kaitlyn and tell her when your flight arrives. She'll come and pick you up. Got all that?"

"Yes."

"Repeat it back to me."

Oliver listened as Ava went through the instructions. "I've never been on a plane before," she said.

"Don't worry, you'll love it. You'll be up in the sky. Above everything. They give you free soft drinks. Ready?"

Ava tilted her blank inscrutable face toward him. "What's in the envelope?" she said.

"Money. It's yours. If they ask at the post office, tell them it's some paperwork."

"But where did it—"

"Ava, you can never tell anyone what happened tonight. You'll be safe, but you can't say a word. Not to anyone. Understand me?"

"Not even Kaitlyn?"

"Not anyone. Not ever."

Oliver waited until she nodded.

"Come on, it's time."

He picked up her suitcase and carried it out and down the steps. She followed, wearing her backpack. The street was threaded through with early morning birdsong and a creeping gray light. He didn't see any neighbors' windows lit up. That was a relief. He pulled the handle up on her rolling bag and scooted it toward her. He stepped in and gave her a quick hug.

"Now go," he said to Ava. "You'll be fine. You're tough."

He pushed her, gently, in the direction she needed to walk and watched until she turned the corner. It was out of his hands now, what happened to her, but he'd done his best. She didn't belong here. She'd be alright back home. Once this was over he'd ensure Lane's estate lawyers found her. He could contact them from prison, if that's how it played out. The house and everything else would be hers.

Oliver turned back to the house and the two dead people inside. His stomach heaved and he vomited in the neighbor's azaleas. He wiped his mouth with the back of his hand, gritted his teeth to keep from screaming. He climbed the steps and went inside, shutting the front door behind him. He walked through each room. There was no sign that Ava had ever been there. Her fingerprints would be everywhere, he supposed, but he doubted she'd have prints on file anywhere.

Lane lay where he'd placed her, on the basement floor. His Lane. He touched her arm, pulled his hand back, tried to breathe, but something wouldn't let him. Oliver thought of his aunt dying in her bed in that Houston apartment with the bad Sheetrock job, the corners misaligned. Not even Houston proper, just a shitty suburb. He finally was able to inhale but the air came out in a sob. He cried for a minute. *Pull it together, asshole,* he said to himself.

He went back upstairs and stood over the corpse in the hallway. Art fucking Guidry. His head spun. He slumped to the wall. He hadn't known the guy would do some shit like this. Guidry had killed Lane, but it was Oliver's fault.

In the costume room he saw Ava had made the bed. Jesus, that kid. He sat on it, then lay down, got under the covers, wrinkled them up. Imagined hearing what she had heard, in the middle of the night. Casting around in the dark for the gun, loading it, tiptoeing out there, terrified. When he'd been her age, he probably would've hid under the bed. He felt like doing that now.

Instead he rehearsed his story. He'd had too much to drink and crashed at Lane's, woke up, heard voices . . . Once they figured out who was lying in the hall, there would be chaos. He'd tell what he knew about Lane and Artie's history, but he'd leave Ava and the blackmail out of it. Whatever happened after would depend on the cops and lawyers.

He got out of the bed, leaving the covers a mess, went to the dining room, and wiped down the gun. He held it, heavy and cold, his finger on the trigger, and tossed it back on the table. In the front room he found his phone and placed two calls. The first was to John, who wouldn't answer because he never turned his ringer on before 8:00 A.M. Oliver left a voicemail: "John, it's me. Listen. Something bad has happened. To Lane. I'm gonna need a lawyer. Can you arrange it? I'll call you back when I can."

He hung up and dialed 911. The operator answered and he said, "Please help me. Someone broke in. My boss is dead. I think I shot someone."

He stayed on the phone with the operator. He gave out the address, tried to answer her questions. He permitted himself a long sip from the whiskey bottle on the floor, and spoke in drunken, gulping sobs. "*I'm sorry,*" he said to the operator. "*What have I done? I'm sorry.*" He held the phone to his ear, listened to her voice, wept. Dawn softened the shadows in the room as he waited for the police to arrive.

CHAPTER 39

Out on the bay, the sailboat scuds along, a slim triangle, a wrist flick of paint. A gestural, painterly rhythm beats through the water and the sky, not stopping at the edges of the forms but continuing the pattern in color. The girl's toes curl in the sand, the tops of her feet brown from the sun. The light plays over her dress, a floral pattern of exquisite detail, tiny pink daisies and bluebonnets tied with red ribbon, row after row of them following the pleats and smocking, the contours of the child's body, the wind blowing the fabric. There is a kind of transference happening, like the sea is made of cloth and the dress of flowered water. Color murmurs through the eddies of blue-brown surf and the folds of the dress as though they are one surface, hiding the same unfathomable depths.

The girl holds out her hand, pinches a live crawfish between her fingers. The creature is a locus of red, a color like nothing else in the landscape. It comes off the wall, or rather, everything else recedes, declines, as in a curtsy. The fingers holding it turn white at the knuckles. The hectic angles of the crawfish's eyestalks and antennae organize the entire beach around it.

Sea oats and palmettos jut in clumps from the dunes. A few

gulls dive. Brown pelicans rest on the pilings of a washed-away pier. Two slashes of paint indicate a great blue heron on the far shore, fishing below a stand of pines. Hermit crabs bury themselves in the sand at Louise's feet and minnows dart in the shallows. Every surface skims a mass of life beneath it.

The house huddles around this girl. It loves her as Lane loved her, helplessly, endlessly, through time and out of it. The painting looks into the room and in looking opens it up. The wall is no longer a wall. It stretches backward to the horizon of this beach and this girlhood. The air in the room relays leaf shadow from the windows and pulls sun from the million fractal surfaces of the bay. Throws beach light onto the hardwood floor, scratched and speckled with paint. The house breathes color and sea air. It keeps the painting safe and waits for Ava.

ACKNOWLEDGMENTS

Enormous gratitude to my New Orleans family and friends, who have welcomed me into their unique versions of the city: Dale Davis, Jennie and Brian Allee-Walsh, Jennette Ginsburg, Pat Galloway and Peter Webb, Beth Davis Poirrier, Noah Tobin, Pableaux Johnson, Everett Bexley, and Jessica Allee-Walsh. Thanks especially to my parents, Betsy and Guss Ginsburg, who raised me on, if not in, New Orleans.

Thank you to Nick Burrell for answering all my questions about mural painting, to Paul Broussard for general expertise and a lovely rainy afternoon at Cane and Table, to Ann Koerner and Dean Coe for advising me about antiques, and to the excellent tour guides at Save Our Cemeteries. Thanks to Becky Homminga for sharing her medical knowledge and for being my second mom.

Thank you to the College of Liberal Arts at the University of Mississippi for funding my research, and to my colleagues in Mississippi's English department for their support and friendship.

To my agent, Duvall Osteen, and my editor, Zack Wagman.

Y'all made this book better than I could have on my own. I'm lucky to work with you.

Thank you to the writers and friends who were kind enough to read and critique early drafts: Kate Lechler, Ivo Kamps, Mary Miller, Ari Friedlander, and especially Chris Offutt, brilliant editor and partner in all things.

Melissa Ginsburg was born and raised in Houston, Texas, and attended the Iowa Writers' Workshop. She is the author of the novel *Sunset City* and the poetry collection *Dear Water Ghost*. She teaches creative writing and literature at the University of Mississippi in Oxford.